Leo (Intergalactic Dating Agency)

Sophie Stern

Published by Sophie Stern, 2022.

Also by Sophie Stern

Alien Chaos
Destroyed
Guarded
Saved
Christmas on Chaos
Alien Chaos: A Sci-Fi Alien Romance Bundle

Aliens of Malum
Deceived: An Alien Brides Romance
Betrayed: An Alien Brides Romance
Fallen: An Alien Brides Romance
Captured: An Alien Brides Romance
Regret
Crazed
For Keeps
Rotten: An Alien Brides Romance

Anchored
Starboard
Battleship
All Aboard
Abandon Ship
Below Deck
Crossing the Line
Anchored: Books 1-3
Anchored: Books 4-6

Ashton Sweets
Christmas Sugar Rush
Valentine's Sugar Rush
St. Patty's Sugar Rush
Halloween Sugar Rush

Bullies of Crescent Academy
You Suck
Troublemaker
Jaded

Club Kitten Dancers
Move

Pose
Climb

Dragon Enchanted
Hidden Mage
Hidden Captive
Hidden Curse

Fate High School
You Wish: A High School Reverse Harem Romance
Freak: A Reverse Harem High School Romance
Get Lost: A Reverse Harem Romance

Good Boys and Millionaires
Good Boys and Millionaires 1
Good Boys and Millionaires 2

Grimalkin Needs Brides
Ekpen (Intergalactic Dating Agency)
Torao (Intergalactic Dating Agency)
Leo (Intergalactic Dating Agency)

Honeypot Babies
The Polar Bear's Baby
The Jaguar's Baby
The Tiger's Baby

Honeypot Darlings
The Bear's Virgin Darling
The Bear's Virgin Mate
The Bear's Virgin Bride

Office Gentlemen
Ben From Accounting

Polar Bears of the Air Force
Staff Sergeant Polar Bear
Master Sergeant Polar Bear
Airman Polar Bear
Senior Airman Polar Bear

Return to Dragon Isle
Dragons Are Forever

Dragon Crushed: An Enemies-to-Lovers Paranormal Romance
Dragon's Hex
Dragon's Gain
Dragon's Rush

Shifters at Law
Wolf Case
Bearly Legal
Tiger Clause
Sergeant Bear
Dragon Law

Shifters of Rawr County
The Polar Bear's Fake Mate
The Lion's Fake Wife
The Tiger's Fake Date
The Wolf's Pretend Mate
The Tiger's Pretend Husband
The Dragon's Fake Fiancée
The Red Panda's Fake Mate

Stormy Mountain Bears
The Lumberjack's Baby Bear
The Writer's Baby Bear
The Mountain Man's Baby Bears

Sweet Nightmares
Sweet Nightmares: The Vampire's Melody
The Sound of Roses

Team Shifter
Bears VS Wolves
No Fox Given

The Fablestone Clan
Dragon's Oath
Dragon's Breath
Dragon's Darling
Dragon's Whisper
Dragon's Magic

The Feisty Dragons
Untamed Dragon
Naughty Dragon
Monster Dragon

The Hidden Planet

Vanquished
Outlaw
Conquered

The Wolfe City Pack
The Wolf's Darling
The Wolf's Mate
The Wolf's Bride

Standalone
Saucy Devil
Billionaire on Top
Jurassic Submissive
The Editor
Alien Beast
Snow White and the Wolves
Kissing the Billionaire
Wild
Alien Dragon
The Royal Her
Be My Tiger
Alien Monster
The Luck of the Wolves
Honeypot Babies Omnibus Edition
Honeypot Darlings: Omnibus Edition
The Swan's Mate

The Feisty Librarian

Polar Bears of the Air Force

Wild Goose Chase

Star Princess

The Virgin and the Lumberjacks

Resting Bear Face

By Hook or by Wolf

I Dare You, King

Shifters at Law

Pretty Little Fairies

Seized by the Dragon

The Fablestone Clan: A Paranormal Dragon-Shifter Romance Collection

Star Kissed

Big Bad Academy

Club Kitten Omnibus

Stormy Mountain Bears: The Complete Collection

Bitten by the Vampires

Beautiful Villain

Dark Favors

Savored

Vampire Kiss

Chaotic Wild: A Vampire Romance

Bitten

Heartless

The Dragon's Christmas Treasure

Out of the Woods

Bullies of Crescent Academy

Craving You: A Contemporary Romance Collection

Chasing Whiskey

The Hidden Planet Trilogy
The Bratty Dom
Tokyo Wolf
The Single Dad Who Stole My Heart
Free For Him
The Feline Gaze
Fate High School
Dragon Beast: A Beauty and the Beast Retelling
Boulder Bear
Megan Slays Vampires
Once Upon a Shift: A Paranormal Romantic Comedy
Red: A Wolf Shifter Romance

Table of Contents

For everyone who loves cats as much as me.

**A planet with more cats than people...
Grimalkin needs brides.**

Chapter 1

Tamara

"The next bridal application session begins in three weeks."

The woman speaking pushes her glasses up her pointy nose. Right away, they slide back down.

She pushes them up again, unbothered.

How much of her day does she spend pushing those glasses back up over and over again? And how much of her time does she spend telling prospective brides that they need to come back again later?

"I need to apply *now*," I tell her insistently, pushing my own glasses back up *my* nose because, yeah, I literally have no room to talk. Slipping on my red-rimmed frames is the highlight of my day now that both of my best friends *and* my grandmother are all gone.

And yes, I realize how sad this is.

I give the lady behind the desk what I hope is a sad, yet firm look. There's no telling whether she'll take pity on me or not, but I *have* to get to Grimalkin. I know perfectly well that I'm running out of time.

I know perfectly well that my friends could be in danger.

The woman presses her lips together as she studies me carefully for a moment.

I don't tell her that I have a prosthetic leg or that sometimes I snore. I don't tell her that two of my best friends are on Grimalkin and that I've completely lost contact with them. These are things she doesn't need to know, but she *does* need to know that I'm very, very desperate because maybe there's something she can do.

Maybe there's a button she can push or a string she can pull.

I'm an idiot, I know, for encouraging Amena to go to Grimalkin so she could "save" Holly. She hasn't come back, and we haven't been able to communicate, and I realize now that the tech equipment we got just wasn't good enough.

Neither one of them has sent word, and I know perfectly well that they wouldn't just stop talking to me unless something was wrong.

Friends don't give up on each other, and they wouldn't have given up on me.

It was talking to Amena's brother before he went off-planet with her mom that made me really understand what's probably been happening.

"Meteor showers," he told me. "They're constantly impacting our communications with Grimalkin. I know my sister like, really wanted to go there, but it was a bad idea. The chances of getting to talk to her are almost zero at this point. The bridal agencies that communicate between planets set up very specific dates and times to communicate so that they aren't impacted by that. Just a random person, though? Good luck ever hearing from her again."

I hate the way I feel when I think about that conversation. He doesn't know anything. He's just Amena's dumb big brother who should have offered to take her to Grimalkin himself.

He didn't, though, and she had to go join the bridal exchange at the Intergalactic Dating Agency.

And now I'm trying to do the same thing.

"I can't do anything about that," the woman frowns at me. "The ship leaving today is full. The ship leaving next week is full, too. We've got a stack of applications this high," she gestures about a foot off the desk, indicating an imaginary pile of paper. "I can't even look at applications for the next three weeks."

I stare at her and bite my tongue, so I don't go crazy and scream at her. I can't wait that long. I can't wait to try to go to Grimalkin.

What if my friends need me?

And I'm certain that they do.

Only, she's not going to budge, and I need a way to get off of this damn rock.

Don't cry.

I can't start crying here. I can't.

"I'm sorry for wasting your time," I finally say. I hate that I've come here only to be told *no*. I hate that she's insistent there's nothing she can do.

"I know everyone wants to marry a big, hunky alien," she says with a gentle shrug. "Some of us just have to wait longer than others."

"It's not that," I say quietly. I decide to be a little bit honest about my motivations even though it's probably a bad idea. "Two of my best friends got sent to Grimalkin through the

Intergalactic Dating Agency's Grimalkin Bridal Exchange," I tell her. I'm not sure why I'm blurting out the truth, but at this point, it can't hurt.

Right?

"I just miss them," I say. "I miss my friends. I know marrying an alien is like, a perk, but...well, I miss them."

She considers this for a long minute.

"So, you don't just want to fuck an alien?"

"No," I whisper. I'm not opposed to the idea. Really, I'm not. I've seen pictures of the men from Grimalkin – the women, too. Every damn person on that planet is big and green and beautiful. I bet they know tricks.

"So, you just want to go, right?"

Why is she asking me?

Does she have an idea?

I nod, and the lady leans forward. She lowers her voice and looks around as though someone could walk by at any moment.

"There's no way I can get you in as a bride right now," she whispers, "but if you're just looking to hitch a ride, then I might be able to help you out."

My heart soars.

Yes!

There might be a chance that I'm going to get to go be with my friends. There *might* be a chance that everything is going to be okay after all.

"You know someone?"

"He can get you onto the ship," she says, nodding. "Then you just have to hide until you arrive on Grimalkin."

She's talking about stowing away. That's what she thinks I should do. She thinks I should sneak onto a ship without permission and hide until I reach Grimalkin. I know that it's a journey that takes a couple of months, but what choice do I have?

"Yes," I say immediately. "What do I need to do?"

AS IT TURNS OUT, STOWING away on a bridal ship is actually a pretty difficult task, especially when you're not familiar with the layout of the ship. The clerk's friend sneaks me on board after I produce payment – two cats from Earth. It's a strange sort of deal, but apparently Earth housecats are a rarity on Grimalkin and are sold to the rich, so they're often used when bartering deals.

Whatever.

My hiding spot is a little closet close to the pods where the brides all sleep, and I manage to make it the entire two-month flight without being spotted. The guy I bribed with cats brings me food and lets me out from time-to-time so I can shower and stretch my legs. He's not a monster, after all, but he always gets really anxious when he lets me out and tries to get me back into my hiding space as soon as possible.

I get it.

He doesn't want to get into trouble for breaking the rules.

Despite the cramped quarters, I survive. Somehow, sitting in a closet with food and books isn't the worst experience of my life. I'm always complaining that I don't have enough time to read.

Now I've got it.

For a little while, I'm quite sure that everything has gone insanely perfectly, but as soon as the ship lands and someone comes to the closet looking for brooms, I'm totally and utterly *caught*.

Just like that.

All that work for nothing.

The man who hid me is long gone with his cats, which means no one has any knowledge of me or where I came from or why I'm on the ship. Two large green men bring me to an equally large green lady who introduces herself as Miss Arieh. She's the one who runs the bridal exchange here on Grimalkin.

She's the one who will decide my fate.

"Please don't send me back," I say quickly. Before she even has a chance to threaten to send me back to Earth, I blurt out the truth. Well, a half-truth. "I need to be here. I have nothing to go back to."

I don't mention my missing leg. I don't mention anything about my friends. I just tell her that I can't go back. No matter what happens next, I need to stay here on Grimalkin. I can't return.

Miss Arieh doesn't exactly take pity on me, but she does consider my words. For a moment, I think she's going to tell the guards who have captured me to just kill me now. I suspect they won't find me worth keeping alive. After all, housing a person costs money.

That's not what she says, though.

"I have no more need for brides at the moment," she tells me. "My grooms are all matched up, but I suppose you can help me around the agency until the next ship arrives."

Is this for real?

The agency on Grimalkin is where the brides come in from Earth. They're trussed up and dressed up and presented to their grooms before they go off onto the planet. This is where Holly and Amena both landed. It's my best starting point for trying to track them and figure out what's happened to them.

And Miss Arieh is going to let me stay.

For now.

"Really?"

She nods. I know that we aren't friends. I know that she's not someone I can trust. All I know is that she's giving me a weird, random chance to at least stay alive for a little while until I can locate my friends.

Until I can have a shot at finding the people I love.

I don't mention this to her. I don't tell her I'm on a strange sort of rescue mission because I know she won't release me into the wild. She's not going to just offer to let me go exploring the planet in search of my buddies. That's not how things work around here. If she even suspects that I know someone on Grimalkin or that I'm going to try to find them, she'll send me right back to Earth because the Grimalkin Bridal Exchange doesn't have time for troublemakers.

"Thank you," I tell her. "I won't let you down."

"That's an odd thing to say," Miss Arieh says with a frown. "I'm not your mother. I don't care if you let me down. I said you can stay for a bit while we wait for the next transport to arrive but trust me when I say that you'll be returning to Earth soon. I can't have a random human running around my building. Not long-term."

My hopes fall just as fast as they rose.

So, I'm not going to be safe here.

I'm going to have to go back unless I can find a way out of this building when she's not looking.

Oh, I'm going to find a damn way.

Chapter 2

Leo

The marriage is something I've been waiting for my entire life but now that it's here, I'm suddenly filled with wild anxiety that I didn't anticipate needing to prepare for.

What if I'm not enough?

What if I'm not good enough for a human?

What if my match doesn't like me?

I have money. I have plenty of money. If I marry a human who likes money, I'll be set. Chances are that she won't even notice the fact that I'm not a *real* Grimalkin.

Chances are that she'll be so distracted by the money that she won't notice my missing tail or the fact that I'm a damn virgin with no real-life experience.

"You okay?" My cousin, Apollo breaks into my thoughts. The two of us are hanging out in my living room and preparing for the short journey to the Intergalactic Dating Agency where the Grimalkin Bridal Exchange is located. It's a program that helps match Grimalkin men with human women from Earth, and they're the ones who are going to decide my fate today.

They're the ones who are going to help me find a bride.

Unlike my brothers, I live close to the agency. I'm only a few blocks away, which means I don't even need to use a hover vehicle to get there.

Instead, my cousin and I are planning on making the walk on foot. It's a pleasant, sunny day, and I always tell myself that I can use the exercise. Getting out and about is one of my favorite things to do, and today is no exception.

Today is the sort of day where I just want to *be*.

Feeling the sun on my skin and having a little bit of time to walk in silence is definitely going to put me in a good mood before I get to the agency. I'm just sure of it.

"I'm fine," I manage to grunt out. I don't want to tell Apollo that I'm having second thoughts about the entire marriage thing.

"You don't seem fine."

"You seem to have a firm grasp on the obvious," I mutter, shaking my head.

"Hey," Apollo frowns. My cousin is something of a silly man. He's very sarcastic and very ridiculous, but he's also soft beneath the jokes and the snarky comments.

And he's not married, either.

Unlike me, Apollo is the oldest brother in his family. There are three of them, and not a single one of them has any interest in marriage.

Yet.

One day, I'm sure they will, but for now, Apollo keeps himself busy and out of trouble. He spends a lot of time helping his mom out since his dad passed away, as well.

"Sorry," I shrug.

"It's okay. I'll just brush it off as you being nervous about the wedding."

"I'm not nervous."

"So, you say. Got the cat?"

I nod and gesture toward a small kitten who is sprawled out on my floor. Why she doesn't climb onto the couch or go into the bedroom and leap up onto the bed, I don't know. My bed hovers a few feet off the ground, but it's cozy as hell, and I know cats well enough to know that if this one wanted to be up there, she would be.

"She looks comfy," Apollo notes.

"That's putting it lightly."

"Where'd you find her?"

"Torao," I tell him.

"Of course. He got in a new collection of cats recently, didn't he?"

"He always does."

My older brother runs this cat palace. He provides space for cats who need homes and lets them live their best damn lives. He's got this sweet, gentle touch where any lost creature can find comfort with him.

Then there's my other brother, Ekpen. He's a bit rougher around the edges. He's kind of big and kind of mean, but his wife, Holly, really helps him stay calm. They're about to have a kid, too, which means that my brother is going to be a dad.

Sometimes it's hard for me to look at them and see just how damn happy they are.

It's hard for me to wonder when it's going to be my time.

I *know* that I'm going to make a great dad, just as I know I'm going to make a great husband. All I need is a little bit of time.

All I need is someone who will be patient with me.

"Woah," Apollo says, bringing me back to the present.

"What?"

"Where did you go just then?"

I stare at him.

"Cousin, I know you just went somewhere in your head. Judging by the look on your face, I'd say that it was someplace dark."

"No," I shake my head. "It's nothing." I reach for a little basket I prepared in advance. It's a deep green that matches my skin.

"There's no way that kitten is going to ride in the basket."

"She will," I insist. "I lined the inside with a soft little blanket." Reaching for the kitten, I prepare to place her in the basket. It's got a cover on top so there's no way she'll be able to jump free as we walk to the Intergalactic Dating Agency, but as it turns out, my cousin knows more than me in this moment because the kitten screeches and runs away.

Apollo grins and shoots me a look that says, "I told you."

Yeah, well, screw that guy.

Together, the two of us manage to catch the kitten. Despite her small size, she's remarkably fast and it takes both of us to collect her. Once she's been properly captured, I place her inside of the basket. She starts meowing loudly, though, obviously protesting her terrible situation. I do feel a little bad for bringing her, but it's tradition.

"It's a bad idea," he tells me, frowning. Apollo gestures to the cat who is meowing wildly.

"What is?"

"Bringing a kitten into the Intergalactic Dating Agency in these conditions. Look how sad this little cat is."

I once again look at the cat, who is still crying like crazy. I wish I could give her a name and promise her that everything's going to be okay, but I can't. That's not how this works.

There are plenty of traditions that are made to be broken, but a bride is supposed to be able to name her own cat.

That's the policy.

"Let's just get this over with," I mutter. I carry the basket with the sad little cat and the two of us leave my house and start walking. We make our way down the road and head straight for the building that's going to change my life. As we walk, the cat starts to calm down. I'm guessing that the rocking motion of the basket is soothing to her.

When we arrive in front of the building, I pause for just a moment outside.

"Are you sure you're ready? You look scared." Apollo grins and crosses his arms over his broad chest. My cousin is nothing if not obnoxious. I know that he's a good man, but right now, I'm not sure why he came. I suppose it's because I wanted someone with me, but I haven't told my brothers yet.

They're both caught up in their own lives and dealing with their own issues.

I didn't want to bother them.

"I'm ready," I tell Apollo. "One hundred percent ready."

It's a total lie.

I'm not ready.

Nothing about this situation is me being "ready."

I'm going to marry someone and make babies with her, but she's…

She's going to have the chance to hurt me, and I'm not sure that I'm ready for this.

I was always the kid who read stories.

I'm the one who used to daydream about falling in love and growing old with someone the way my parents have.

I'm not the kid who gets the girl.

"Then let's go," Apollo says, and we head inside. We walk straight ahead to where an android is sitting in the center of the room. Its face is strangely blank, but I'm pretty sure I'm supposed to talk to this robot. A quick glance around reveals that there's no one else here, and I do have an appointment.

"Hello," I say.

The android stays quiet.

The rest of the room is completely empty. There's just this android standing in the center of the room.

I look at Apollo, but he only shrugs. He doesn't know, either.

"Hello," I say again. This time, I speak a bit louder.

"It's broken," a friendly voice says. I turn to see a wall lifting up. Miss Arieh, the woman who runs the Intergalactic Dating Agency is standing there with a big smile. "I'm so sorry, gentlemen. It's something I've been meaning to repair but haven't." She steps forward and offers a small wave. "Leo, it's good to see you." She turns to Apollo and cocks her head. "And I don't believe I've met you."

"Apollo," my cousin says.

"I'm Miss Arieh. Apollo, are you ready to sign up to meet your mate?"

He shakes his head instantly, letting her know that he's not interested at all, but I notice something that Miss Arieh doesn't.

I see the way Apollo's tail swishes behind him. It's just the slightest little movement, just the tiniest gesture that lets me know he is, in fact, interested in meeting a mate.

Interesting.

I had no idea until today that my darling cousin was ready to find his own wife. Perhaps there will be more weddings on Grimalkin before the month is over.

"Well," she shrugs. "You know where to come when you're ready. I run the Grimalkin Bridal Exchange here at the Intergalactic Dating Agency. It's my job to match Grimalkin men with women from Earth."

"What about the Grimalkin women?" Apollo asks. "There are still some Grimalkin women. Do you arrange spouses for them?"

She shakes her head. "That's a different program. Grimalkin women also have the opportunity to mate with someone from on-planet."

It's just that we have so many men here. Almost every Grimalkin child really is a man, which makes it absolutely vital for our survival to marry people from off-planet.

And that's why I'm here.

Miss Arieh seems to be done speaking to Apollo because she turns back to me and looks me up and down. I'm wearing a simple black shirt and black pants. My cousin is dressed identically to me. The only difference is that his tail is sticking out of the back of his pants, while mine isn't because I don't have a tail.

Not anymore.

Miss Arieh doesn't notice or doesn't comment, which I appreciate. There's nothing quite as terrible as seeing someone glance to the spot where my tail *should* be and then realizing it's not there at all.

"It's time," she says.

She turns around and walks forward. A moment later, Miss Arieh presses her hand to the wall and moves it in a pattern that looks random to me, but that I assume is well practiced. The wall slides up and there stands a woman who is tall and curvy with long red hair. It falls past her shoulders in thick waves. She grins. The smile lights up her whole face.

"This is Kate," Miss Arieh says with a smile. She gestures to me. "And this is Leo. He's your groom."

I smile at Kate but feel nothing when I look at her. She's a beautiful human, to be sure. Her face is pretty and covered in tiny freckles. She's adorable, really, but she's...

Well, she's not who I would have pictured as my mate.

"Hello, Kate," I say, stepping forward.

She stares at me curiously. She doesn't look happy to see me at first. I wonder if she's as disappointed with this arrangement as I am.

Not that I'm *disappointed.*

It's just that, well, this isn't really how I saw this entire thing *going.*

I kind of thought that I'd show up today and the woman Miss Arieh chose for me would be the perfect fit, only it seems a little bit awkward.

Apollo, however, does not seem to feel the same way.

He steps in front of me and walks toward Kate.

"Kate," he says, stopping directly in front of her. He's between the two of us, so I can't even see her anymore. Miss Arieh starts protesting as Apollo lowers his head to Kate's and starts kissing her right in the middle of the room.

I choke back a chuckle.

Okay, so Kate's going to be getting married today.

Just not to me.

When Apollo finally pulls away, Kate shakes her head.

"I'm so confused," she whispers. "I thought I was supposed to marry...the other one."

Miss Arieh glares at Apollo and then turns to me.

"He hasn't gone through the processing yet. We haven't done the paperwork!"

"Then get it started," I shrug. "I'm sure you can find me another match who will be more appropriate for me."

"It's not that simple," she glares.

"Make it simple."

It's obvious that Kate and Apollo have an instant connection, and there's no way in hell I'm going to stand between that. Kate is wildly beautiful and while Apollo isn't ready for a wife at *all*, I know he'll be good to her. He's got a gaggle of younger brothers who will not be eligible to take their own wives, as well, and they'll be thrilled.

Reluctantly, Miss Arieh disappears and comes back with a tablet. She starts walking Apollo through all of the paperwork he needs to complete. Then she performs the short and sweet marriage ceremony. Then they're ready to leave.

"Wait," Apollo says. "I don't have a cat."

I hand him the little basket with the tiny white cat inside of it.

"Are you sure?" Apollo asks me. "What about your bride?"

"I'll visit Torao," I shrug. "I'm sure I'll be able to find a new cat."

I can find something better. This kitty is sweet but judging by the way Kate is looking at it, I know that she's going to be the best one to take care of it.

"I owe you," Apollo tells me, and then him and Kate disappear out of the building and start walking off down the road.

As soon as we're alone, Miss Arieh glares at me.

"I hope you're happy."

"What?"

"That was *your* bride, Leo. That's the woman I chose for you."

"You chose wrong," I shrug. "I'm sure it's happened before."

"No." Miss Arieh shakes her head, and I suddenly realize that she's completely baffled by this situation. "It has *never* happened, Leo. I never make mistakes. I never have a mismatch. You are the very first groom to ever have a problem with the bride I've chosen."

I hesitate, but finally ask.

"Do you have any spare brides around today?"

She sighs. "I don't have any extra brides. I match everyone before they even come to Grimalkin. In fact, it's only brides who are the passengers on the ships. Everyone else is the crew. Except for-"

Suddenly, she stops, and I realize that there's something else she was about to say.

"What is it?"

"There was a stowaway," she says slowly, looking back at me. "On this last shipment. She's not the woman I would have chosen for a strong Grimalkin mate. In fact, I'm not even sure if she can have children. We haven't run any testing. We haven't done bloodwork."

I know why Miss Arieh is nervous about this. The entire purpose of the Grimalkin Bridal Exchange at the Intergalactic Dating Agency is to ensure that each Grimalkin man is able to reproduce with his chosen mate.

"I want to see her," I say firmly.

Suddenly, without knowing anything else except for the fact that Miss Arieh views her as "broken," I want to meet this woman. I want to have a chance of my own to talk to her and to look at her and to see if she's just the right woman for me because something deep inside of me tells me that she definitely, totally is.

"I want to see her," I repeat.

"She didn't come here as a bride."

"I don't care. Let me meet her."

Miss Arieh stares at me.

"I've matched your entire family, Leo," she says. She means my brothers and now my cousin. My parents met naturally, which is strange to think about since that so rarely happens now.

"I understand this."

"I've matched your entire family and I've never been wrong."

I take a step forward and look at the woman who pours her heart and soul into making love happen. She does everything she can to make sure that every single person in the world falls deeply, madly in love with their paramours.

"Choose love today," I tell her. "Let me meet this woman."

Chapter 3

Tamara

Grimalkin isn't so bad and being a prisoner isn't nearly as terrible as I thought it was going to be. I'm fed a weird meal of purple stew and green fruit. It's a weird combination, but it doesn't taste bad. The soup, I'm told, is from the planet Malum. The fruit is native to Grimalkin.

Who knew that a cat planet would have so many tasty options?

I've never been scared of food or of trying new things. The truth is that for me, food has always been something I've been worried about. Growing up, I didn't have a lot. Once I lost my leg, the medical bills piled up and food became even more scarce.

My grandmother did her best, but sometimes that just wasn't enough.

I don't want to think about the fact that she's gone now or the fact that my two best friends are somewhere on this planet alone. I don't know what's happened to them or where they've gone.

All I know is that right now, they're my only reason for living.

I finish my food quietly and then continue sitting still. I'm in a room that has no doors and no windows. There's no way for me to escape. This building is kind of strange because the only way to get in or out is to know the pattern to draw on the walls, and that's not something I know how to do.

So, I sit.

And I wait.

And I wonder what's going to happen to me.

I don't have to wonder for long because it's only a few minutes before the wall slides open and Miss Arieh, the woman who placed me here with my bowl of soup, appears.

She glides into the room, rather than walking, and sits down across from me.

"Tamara."

That one word gives me so much anxiety that I don't know what to do.

Why is she saying my name like this?

What exactly am I in trouble for now?

"That's my name," I whisper, echoing a phrase my grandmother used to say. I leave off the "don't wear it out" bit.

"I need a bride," she says.

"Excuse me?"

"I need a bride."

"Um..." I look around. What is she talking about? Is she asking me to be a bride or to help her find one? Because I'm not sure that I can do either of those things.

Miss Arieh is beautiful, and she's exactly the type of woman I've gone for in the past. I've never been particularly concerned about whether the person I date is a man or a woman. I've always just cared about having a connection.

But is Miss Arieh asking *me* to be *her* bride?

"I need a bride," she repeats.

Okay, yeah. She's definitely proposing.

"Are you proposing to me?" I ask her, needing to be sure. I'm not sure if this would be a good time for me to say yes. I mean, it would give me a good reason to stay on Grimalkin. I could get married and then snoop around and try to find out what happened to my friends.

Miss Arieh's dark green skin seems to pale as she shakes her head.

"Oh no," she says. "Oh no."

Okay, yeah, so I read *this* situation completely wrong. Embarrassment washes over me as I realize that I've screwed up entirely.

Shit.

Shit, shit, shit.

This *so* isn't what I need right now. My entire purpose of coming here was to blend in and find a way to make myself invisible so I could snoop around and find my buddies.

Apparently, that's not in the cards for me.

So, I'd better get used to things like being alone or living on a ship because I have a really big feeling that Miss Arieh is about to send me right back to Earth.

"Not me," Miss Arieh says. "I have a man."

"A man?"

"A man."

She pauses, hesitating, and I wonder what the story is here. Is this a guy that everyone hates? Like, is he some sort of unlikable dude?

Or maybe he's a villain.

Is he a murderer?

Am I going to have to sleep with a murderer in order to find my friends?

I realize that Miss Arieh is asking me to do something for her, which means this could be my only chance at bargaining for information. I don't want to push her too hard because I'm pretty sure she's one wrong word away from sending me back to Earth, but I do think I need to ask.

"Miss Arieh?"

She stares, raising a perfectly shaped green eyebrow.

"If I stay here, will I ever be able to talk to people back on Earth?"

"No," she says quickly.

Too quickly.

Is this a question that has been asked before?

"No? Why not? It's not allowed?"

She sighs. "Grimalkin is a strange planet, Tamara. I can communicate with Earth from here just fine, but this is one of the only places on the damn planet where there's a clear line of communication."

"What do you mean?"

"I mean that we're far away. Even I have static and disconnections when I try to reach Earth. Even I have a hard time staying in touch sometimes depending on whether there are meteor showers happening anywhere between Grimalkin and Earth."

"But you can still communicate with Earth."

"Most people don't have the level of technical equipment that I do," she shrugs. "While talking to people back on Earth isn't forbidden, it's nearly impossible."

The devices.

The devices my friends sneaked here.

I left mine behind when I tried to come to Grimalkin. Both Amena and Holly brought their devices and although we had the briefest of interactions after they left, there was little chance of me being able to sneak my communication device on board the ship with me.

I already hobble a little bit because of my prosthetic leg. Most of the time, I'm great about blending in. Unless I tell someone, "Hey, I don't have a leg," they usually don't put it all together.

But having a forbidden device on board the transport vessel is a huge no-no, and I didn't want that counting against me more.

"So, if I marry this man," I say slowly.

"You likely won't be able to talk to anyone back on Earth," she says. "Unless he's quite wealthy and has incredible communication tech, which I doubt."

"Why's that?"

"Because most of the men on Grimalkin like hanging out with their cats more than they like talking to people back on Earth," she tells me. "So, what do you say? Do you want to get married today?"

Do I even really have a choice?

Chapter 4

Leo

I wait in the empty room long after Apollo and Miss Arieh leave.

I'm not even the slightest bit sad that Apollo took Kate and ran off with her. My cousin deserves to be happy, and Kate deserves to have a life that makes her feel incredible.

But then the walls slide up and I turn to see the most beautiful woman I've ever seen in my life.

This.

This is the girl for me.

She's got black skin and short hair. She's got these deep brown eyes that I can just see myself drowning in. Her glasses have red frames, and they match the floor-length red dress she's wearing.

I don't know who the hell she is, but she's mine.

I know it deep in my soul.

This is the feeling I was missing with Kate.

This is the emotion I needed to feel but didn't.

"Mine," I say, walking forward. I stride across the room to her. Before Miss Arieh can start complaining about the proper procedure for today, I tug the woman into my arms, and I kiss her.

She's tense and probably scared. After all, coming to live on an alien planet can't be an easy experience, but it doesn't matter. None of it matters because the second our lips touch, she melts against me.

She groans, wrapping her arms around my neck, and I know.

I know that she's just the one for me.

As expected, Miss Arieh dislikes this turn of events and starts complaining right away about the fact that the two of us are touching each other, but I don't care.

I need her.

I want her.

I *crave* her.

"Seriously," Miss Arieh's voice becomes sharper and clearer, pulling me from the lust-induced haze I'm in. "Leo, stop it now or I'll call your mother."

Not the police.

My mother.

I turn, glaring at Miss Arieh. I don't know this woman very well at all, but she's starting to really piss me off.

"My mother?"

She nods.

"Do you think I'm scared of Mommy?" I ask, raising an eyebrow.

Miss Arieh instantly realizes that she's got me all wrong. I may be the baby of the family, but my mother has never been the kind of woman to play favorites or to overreach with her parenting boundaries.

When I left home, she set me free.

She's not the kind of woman who's going to come here and try to stop my damn wedding from happening.

Turning back to the woman I'm holding in my arms, I smile.

"My name is Leo," I tell her. "Will you marry me?"

Then I hold my breath because whatever her answer is, it's going to change everything.

Chapter 5

Tamara

He's asking.

He's giving me a choice.

He cares about me and what I think and he's giving me a damn choice. He's giving me something I haven't been given in a long time.

Maybe ever.

"Oh," I whisper.

He looks hopeful.

Excited.

Curious.

When was the last time anyone was *curious* about me? Holly, Amena, and I have our share of ex-girlfriends and ex-boyfriends who broke our hearts and made us cry, but this guy is different. This guy will be *devastating* if he ever decides to walk away.

I should say no.

I should forget about my friends, tell him no, and retreat back to Earth with my tail between my legs like a little puppy dog because this giant of a man is too much.

He's scary, really.

He's a damn giant.

Still, there's something about him that makes me really, really want to say yes.

There's something about him that makes me want to give this thing between us a chance, and so when I open my mouth again, the word that tumbles out is, "yes."

Yes, I will marry this alien.

He grins boyishly, and I get the feeling that he was strangely worried I'd say no. Since I'm a backup bride of some sort, I'm not sure why he would be worried, but I won't complain.

Miss Arieh performs the perfunctory marriage ceremony. Leo frowns at me as we complete the ceremony. I don't realize why at first, but then he turns to Miss Arieh.

"I'll get her a bracelet and a cat on the way home," he tells her.

"See that you do."

Miss Arieh turns to me and looks me up and down. She let me choose the long red dress because it covers my prosthetic quite well, but I know that sooner or later, this guy is going to figure out that I'm not what I pretend to be.

Then Miss Arieh leaves. She does her weird wall magic stuff. I still don't really understand the different patterns she runs over the steel walls to make them rise and lower, but I suppose that doesn't really matter.

I'm alone now with this man.

My husband.

Leo.

There's a weird-looking android in the center of the room that seems to be watching us, but I try to ignore it and instead just look at Leo.

"Bracelet?" I ask. And did he say he was going to get me a cat?

As in, a live cat?

"Ah," he says, smiling at me. "They didn't teach you about our customs before you arrived. Did they?"

"No." I don't mention this is because I'm a literal stowaway who isn't supposed to be here. He doesn't need to know *that*.

"Strange," he shrugs. He doesn't seem bothered, nor does he seem interested in explaining.

Instead of offering me more information, he just tugs me close and kisses me again.

This time, he deepens the kiss so much that I feel like I'm in a head spin.

This guy is making me dizzy, and he's making my girl parts spring to life in ways they haven't in a very, very long time.

When was the last time I felt like this?

I can't even remember.

"What are you doing to me?" I whisper.

He cups my cheek and strokes my skin softly.

"You're beautiful, Tamara," he says. Then he presses his lips to my forehead. "Come on. Let's get you a bracelet."

Chapter 6

Leo

We leave the Intergalactic Dating Agency office and start walking toward my house. My plan is to buy her a bracelet, take her home, and spend the whole evening getting to know her. At some point, we'll go to Torao's place so she can pick out a cat of her own.

My brother definitely has more than enough cats. He won't mind sharing one with us. In fact, that's the entire reason he runs his "cat palace," as he calls it.

"Why did you come to Grimalkin?" I ask Tamara. I sound a little gruffer than I mean to. I realize I've messed up when she stiffens at my words.

"I...what?"

I hate that I'm screwing this up. There's a reason I'm a doctor and not a customer service specialist. I'm good at fixing things that are broken. I'm not good at softening my words. That's the problem with me, isn't it?

I've never been as tough as Ekpen or as charming as Torao. Both of my older brothers have been these strong giants for as long as I can remember, but me...

Well, I'm just me.

I'm not anyone especially special.

"Why did you choose this planet?" I ask her, trying to rephrase my question so she understands what I mean. I know that sometimes, trying to communicate with humans isn't just about language. She has her language processing chip, so she can understand me, but...

Well, there's more to communication than speaking the same language.

"I heard a lot of good things about it," Tamara tells me.

"Like what?" She doesn't seem to know a lot about our customs, so I'm not sure how much she really knows.

"Like I know that you have a lot of cats here," she says, gesturing to two little black cats who are hanging out in front of a shop. There's a bowl of food set out for them and there seems to be a water fountain installed.

Shopkeepers on Grimalkin care a lot about the animals who live here with us. We all do. One of the reasons our planet is so special is that there are many different cats who are native to the planet, but there are also cats who seek refuge here.

"How many cats do you have on Grimalkin, anyway?"

"A lot."

"How many?"

"Nobody knows. Our planet is smaller than yours, but there is still plenty of room for cats."

"This city," Tamara gestures to the buildings we're passing. They're all quite small – one- and two-story shops – and each one is locally owned and managed. "Is this your capital city?"

"It is," I nod.

"It seems small."

"It is," I agree.

"Doesn't your government need larger buildings?"

She's so curious. I like it. She's asking questions I don't often think about, but that's okay. She's giving me a chance to share my world with her and this is something that I'm enjoying quite a bit.

"There are a few larger buildings where government officials manage our planet," I explain, "but not a lot goes wrong on Grimalkin."

"How is that possible?"

I shrug. "We're a cat planet. We don't bother people. We just take care of the creatures, and we take care of our planet."

We stay out of trouble. We don't get involved in a lot of conflicts. We don't have many enemies.

We're just...us.

"So, are there a lot of cities on Grimalkin?"

"Some," I shrug. "Most of the brides who come through the IDA bridal exchange program here on Grimalkin stay in this city, though."

"Really?"

"Yes. There are other cities sprinkled throughout the planet and some of our citizens choose to live in the woods." Like my cousins. "But for the most part, people who come here as brides live in this place."

"Interesting," she comments.

And I think, for a second, that her mind goes somewhere else.

I want to ask her what she's thinking about and what the real reason is that she came to Grimalkin.

Is she running from something?

Is she in danger?

Before I can pry, though, we arrive at a sweet little bracelet shop where we can buy her a wedding bracelet that will enable her to communicate with me and anyone else on-planet that she wants to. It'll also enable her to do things like spend money and unlock the house. It's an important item for any Grimalkin bride to have, and I'm happy to be able to pick one out *with* her.

"What is this place?" Tamara asks as we stop in front of the shop.

"It's a bracelet shop."

"Bracelet?"

Tamara doesn't know about bracelets. She doesn't know about the geography of our planet. She doesn't know how many cats there are, and she doesn't know our marriage customs.

So, why did she tell me that she chose Grimalkin on purpose?

And why do I suddenly not believe her?

Chapter 7

Tamara

I know.

I know I'm asking too many questions.

I know it's too much.

I know it's too fast.

I just also know that I want him more than I've ever wanted anyone, and I hate myself for it. My only real goal here is to find my besties. I need to make sure they're safe. Once I find them, I'll rescue them and the three of us can go find some random planet to live out our days on together. We need to be saved and we need to have a place where we aren't living our lives in fear.

Although now that I'm here, Grimalkin doesn't seem nearly as frightening as I imagined it would be.

Leo looks at me curiously, and I realize I've most likely screwed up by not knowing what a bridal bracelet is. Damn. I told him I planned to come here because I heard so many great things, but then I didn't even know what this special bracelet thing is.

Awesome.

He stares at me for a moment, and then he smiles.

"It marks you," he says.

"Marks me?"

"As mine."

And just like that, I'm losing myself to this dumb fantasy. I'm losing myself into this idea that I'm something special or that I deserve to be here because I know more than anything that I don't.

I don't deserve to be here with him.

Leo is this big, green man. I wonder if he has scales and a tail like the other Grimalkins that I've caught sight of. Since we've been walking to the bracelet shop, I've seen people jogging on the cobblestone roads just like people jogged back on Earth.

Well, the pollution is bad enough these days that most people on Earth don't jog a lot.

The people here do.

And the air is so damn fresh that it feels like when I was a kid. I used to love running around in the summertime and just breathing in all of the air, and I'm doing that again right now.

"You're so beautiful," Leo murmurs, and then he leans down and kisses me again.

Just like the first time, I'm delighted with the experience. I push up on my toes and wrap my arms around him, pulling him close to me.

And I just breathe him in.

Leo kisses differently than anyone I've ever been with. Most of my former partners have been all about the tongue action – licking, swirling, sucking.

Not Leo.

He uses every part of his mouth to dominate me. Each time I think I'm getting used to the way he's kissing, he mixes it up, nipping at my lips, softly pressing his against mine, and then pulling away to grin at me.

That smile is going to be the death of me.

I'm wearing panties, but I wish I wasn't because they're completely soaked now. Who knew I was going to become completely enamored with this guy?

Who knew that someone like Leo was going to be my utter undoing?

And then, before I can say anything, before my mind catches up with the moment we're sharing, I feel myself slipping. I'm not used to standing on the cobblestone roads here on Grimalkin, and I lose my balance and start to stumble. Right away, I know I'm going to be in trouble as I make my way down to the ground.

I close my eyes and brace for impact, but it never comes.

I don't hit the ground.

I don't land on my ass or my elbows or my back because Leo is bigger than me, and stronger than me, and he catches me before anything goes terribly wrong.

And he looks at me with a curious expression.

"You fell."

"I fell," I whisper.

Don't say it.

Don't say it, I silently urge.

Just.

Don't.

Say.

Anything.

"Are you all right?" Leo asks, but I can't hold it in any longer.

"I only have one leg, okay? I only have one leg."

Chapter 8

Leo

Words can't express how scared I am when Tamara starts to fall. I know that everyone on Grimalkin thinks our roads are so pretty – and they are – but they're also not as safe as the older generation likes to think.

Pretty roads aren't always the same as functional roads, and when it comes to our citizens who use wheelchairs or who struggle to get along without external assistance, it can be rough.

I catch Tamara easily. Her glasses go flying off her head, but she doesn't even notice before she starts talking about how she only has one leg.

"You only have one leg?" I ask, looking down at the luscious human in my arms. I want her. I want her more than I've ever wanted anyone before, but I, too, am missing things.

Experience.

My tail.

Hope.

There's a lot that could go wrong with a guy like me, but there's a deep-rooted part of me that really, really hopes she's going to take a chance on me.

We are married, after all.

"I only have one leg," she says again. "My prosthetic slipped on the cobblestone."

"These damn roads," I mutter, tugging her closer to me. I breathe in, smelling her hair, trying to get a whiff of her soft scent that's so damn alluring. Then I place her carefully on her feet and make sure she can stand okay. Then I drop down and find her glasses. They appear to be unharmed, so I place them back on her head.

"Well?" Tamara asks, placing her hands on her hips.

"What?"

"Aren't you going to ask me?"

Ask her?

Sometimes humans really are confusing.

What am I supposed to be asking her?

I open my mouth and decide that honesty will be the best way for me to deal with this strange, unusual situation.

"What do you want me to ask you, Tamara?"

She seems surprised by this, but she blurts out her answer.

"Aren't you going to ask me why I'm missing a leg?"

No.

I was never going to ask her that.

"I'm sure if you want me to know, you'll tell me."

"That's it?" Tamara gawks.

"That's it. Now, would you like to come inside the shop and choose your bracelet?"

She hesitates for just a moment before she starts nodding and shuffles into the store with me. The two of us are instantly overwhelmed with bright lights and six different cats who scurry over and start meowing at us.

"Whose cats are these?" Tamara asks.

"Mine," a friendly voice says, coming forward. It's Mrs. Oscar, the bracelet shop owner. "Leo? I'm surprised to see you so soon." She turns to Tamara. "You didn't like the bracelet, dear?"

"What?"

Before Tamara can explain that I haven't actually given her one, I jump in.

"As it turns out, Mrs. Oscar, my cousin needed that bracelet more than me."

"Apollo?"

"Yes."

She laughs. "Of course, it was Apollo. The brute. Well, then, come on in and let's find a nice bracelet for you," Mrs. Oscar says to Tamara.

My bride looks to me nervously.

"Are you sure? These all look really-"

"Expensive?" Mrs. Oscar interrupts. "They are. Don't worry, dear. He can afford it."

Chapter 9

Tamara

When we arrive back at Leo's house, he takes me into the little cottage he lives in. It's actually a really cute little place with just one bedroom, one bathroom, and one main room for living in. We passed quite a few larger homes on the way here, but I'm not that kind of girl.

Small is good, in my opinion.

I can deal with small.

"It's not much," he says to me.

"It's perfect."

We go inside and he shows me around. Leo lives close to where he works, so he usually walks. Sometimes he takes the car, which hovers above the ground even when it's not in use. I'm fascinated by this and I kind of want to learn how to drive it, but I'm not brave enough to ask yet.

Once I figure out how to get around Grimalkin, I can start looking for my friends. I don't have a way to communicate with anyone back on Earth, but with my communications bracelet, maybe I can find a way to locate Amena and Holly. If they're both actually married to Grimalkin men now, maybe they have bracelets like mine.

And if they have bracelets like mine, maybe we can call each other.

Leo shows me his little book collection and he introduces me to his three cats: Henry, Oliver, and Preston.

"Those are Earth names," I point out, surprised. Not only are they Earth names, but they're *human* names. I kind of feel like this is strange. Most of the time, people name cats things like "Snowball" or "Princess."

It's not often that Earthlings name their pets things they'd name a person.

"What can I say?" Leo shrugs. "I like Earth."

"Do you?"

"Yes."

"Why?"

"There's so much to love about Earth," he smiles. "And I had the chance to study there while I was training to be a doctor."

"You studied on Earth?"

He nods and grins. "I work with cats mostly, but I got to help examine humans at a clinic."

"You examined humans?"

He nods, and I burst out laughing. When he frowns, I feel forced to explain.

"I'm sorry, it's just that humans are often scared that we're all going to be abducted and examined by aliens. Then you came to Earth and actually did just that."

"I didn't abduct anyone."

My story seems to hurt his feelings, and I placed my hand on his arm.

"I know," I tell him. "And I'm sorry."

He shrugs, but I can tell that he's not feeling as playful as he was earlier. That's okay because I'm not feeling that playful, either. I'm still feeling a little embarrassed about the whole falling-down-in-front-of-him thing, but there's more to my problem than that.

Leo might be okay with the fact that I'm human. He might be okay with the fact that I'm missing a leg. Is he going to be okay with the rest of me, though?

There don't seem to be racial tensions here on Grimalkin. I don't get the impression that he's going to be sad he got me instead of some skinny little white girl. I'm not skinny. I'm not white. He seems perfectly attracted to me physically.

What about when he finds out I've been with women in the past though? Is he going to care that I'm not straight? Not celibate?

Grimalkin seems like it's kind of a traditional place, which might be a problem because I'm not a traditional sort of girl.

I'm not the girl who has been sitting around waiting for her Prince Charming.

I'm the girl who stands up for my friends and who goes to fight for everything they need.

"Are you disappointed with me?" I ask him. I don't really know what happened. I just know that his original bride fell through somehow.

He strokes my cheek, looking down at me.

"Trust me, darling. I could never be disappointed in you."

Then he kisses me.

Just like the other times, I'm completely swept away with his kisses. I'm enamored. I shouldn't be allowing myself to feel this deep attraction to Leo, but I do.

I don't know anything about him except that for someone who claims to be a doctor, he seems to live a simple life.

He tugs me a little bit closer and wraps his arms more tightly around me.

"You're perfect," he murmurs.

"I'm not," I laugh, pulling away. I gesture down. "No leg, Leo. Remember?"

"Stop talking about that," he shakes his head. "I don't care. You don't need to have two legs for me to want you."

I look at him.

Seriously?

This guy can't be for real.

Really, he just can't.

"You don't care that I can't run? Can't go mountain climbing with you?"

"Baby, if you want to run, I'll carry you. If you want to go mountain climbing, I'll carry you on my back."

"I'm way too heavy for that."

"Don't underestimate me, darling," he laughs, but it's a dark sort of laugh. "I'm much stronger than I look."

I don't doubt it.

I know that he's strong.

I know that he's tough.

I just also don't want to be a burden to him.

It doesn't matter, I remind myself silently. *You're only here to find Amena and Holly. This guy doesn't matter.*

Only, he kind of does.

Nobody has ever told me that it doesn't matter before.

Nobody has ever *not* cared about my missing limb.

Only him.

Only Leo.

And I'm suddenly torn because I'm only supposed to be here to find my friends and rescue them if they need me, but I'm suddenly experiencing all of these different feelings and I don't know what to do about them.

Suddenly, the only thing I want is to stay right where I am and just keep kissing Leo.

But I know that it can't happen.

And it's kind of breaking my heart a little bit.

Chapter 10

Leo

I don't want to tell my brothers I'm married.

Not just yet.

A call to Apollo goes unanswered.

Jerk.

He's probably making sweet, sweet love to his new bride. I'm still not really sure how he quite literally managed to steal himself a wife, but it's not my job to know. It's my job to make sure that the wife I *did* end up with knows how loved and adored and wonderful she is.

And oh, this is a human who hasn't felt a lot of love.

We sit down together to eat a simple meal of bread and stew.

"What is with this place and stew?" Tamara asks, looking up at me. I feel just the slightest bit bad. Maybe she doesn't like stew. She reaches for me, though, squeezing my hand. "It's just a question. I *love* soup," she tells me gently. "Love it. My grandmother and I used to make soups and stews every week. It's just not often that I meet other people who like the same thing, and now I've had it twice in one day."

"Grimalkin can get cold in the winter," I shrug. "It's something many of us enjoy when it's cold outside."

"Well, it's pretty nice today," she says. "But I'm glad we're having it anyway."

"This is a garden stew," I explain, trying not to feel hurt at her earlier comment. I don't need to be overly sensitive with this human. I talk her through my cooking methods, and she seems interested enough. When we're finished, I take her to the bedroom.

She turns and looks at me.

"Are you coming to bed with me?"

And this is the part that always trips me up.

I'm not weird.

I have to remind myself that I'm not weird.

Only, I feel a little weird and I also feel slightly uncomfortable. I've never been with a woman *that* way, and I don't really want Tamara to feel like she has to do anything in order to be welcome here.

We have an arranged marriage, which basically means that our union is only designed so we can make babies. Obviously, sex is a part of that. It doesn't have to be tonight, though.

Oh, I really, really want it to be tonight.

She'll have to see me, though.

All of me.

And she'll have to see the tail.

Well, the lack of tail.

Is that really something I'm ready for?

I'm just not sure.

"No," I finally say. I could lie to her. I could make up something about how Grimalkins never have sex on their wedding night. She doesn't know *anything* about our planet, so she'd definitely buy it. Only, I can't bring myself to lie to her.

I can bring myself to hide the truth, obviously, but an outright lie feels cruel and unnecessary.

"Oh," she says. I can tell by the look on her face that she's hurt. She thinks I don't like her because of her leg, but I don't give a shit about that.

Reaching for her chin, I force her to look up at me.

"You're perfect," I say, "but it's been a long day."

For everyone.

"I know," she whispers, "but I thought we could…"

She licks her lips. She wants me as much as I want her.

She wants to make love to me and oh, I want her to be my first.

Still, I need…

Well, I need a little bit of time.

"Goodnight, little human," I murmur. I kiss her, and then I press a button on the wall so the door between us lowers.

It's time for me to go.

Chapter 11

Tamara

Leo is being really weird. He's giving me the craziest hot-and-cold vibes that anyone has given me *ever*, and I don't particularly know what to do about it.

Oh, I know how guys like him operate.

I know that he's probably playing hard to get.

Maybe he wants to be seduced.

Or maybe he doesn't like me.

No, it's not that. I enjoyed kissing him and judging by the hard length of his cock pressing against my tummy while we were kissing, I know he likes me, too.

So, what is it?

What is his deal?

I know he's not holding back because of religious reasons or because he doesn't like me, so...

What could it be?

I'm alone in the bedroom now. It's strange, really. I don't expect to be spending our first night as a husband-and-wife duo alone, yet here I am.

Alone.

Strange.

I try not to feel hurt as I turn to look at the little bedroom. It's nothing fancy or over-the-top, but that's okay. I don't need fancy. I don't need wild or crazy. I just need him.

Leo is a really cool person. I'm still not really sure how I managed to end up mated to someone like him, but here I am.

Mated.

Married.

I'm a wed woman, and there's a part of me that wishes my grandmother was around to see it.

She was still alive when Holly left. She was still around, and I couldn't leave her. It's easy to feel regrets surrounding the fact that my friends left Earth.

Should I have gone with them?

Sometimes, I think that I should have.

Sometimes I think that I should have just sucked it up and left at the same time that they all did because if I'd left, then none of us would have been separated. We would all be together here on Grimalkin and I...

Well, I wouldn't be spending my wedding night alone in a stranger's room.

There's a bed floating in the center of the room. I step forward and take a better look at it. The entire thing is huge. It's bigger than the king size bed my granny used to have, so that's saying something. It's much too big for just one person. Does Leo really need all of this room?

There are blankets and pillows on the bed and one of them moves. That's when I realize that I'm not so alone after all.

There are cats here.

Lots and lots of cats.

I count four cats right away, but there are probably more hiding. I should probably be judgmental and annoyed. After all, four cats is a lot, but I'm not bothered at all. In fact, I think it's sweet that Leo has so many little animals at his home.

There's an attached bathroom, so I go in there and get cleaned up. I'm tired and could use a shower. Plus, I want to get out of the ballgown.

I don't have any extra clothes and it doesn't really look like Leo has anything for me to wear. I rifle through his stuff and manage to find this big, oversized sweatshirt.

Perfect.

When I peer at the shower, I realize there's a bench inside there. Perfect. I can shower without my prosthesis, which is great for me. I remove my leg, sit down on the bench, and let the water pour over me as I wonder what the hell I'm going to do next.

I've got a hot, sexy alien hanging out in the next room and I'm in here alone with a bunch of cats.

The water doesn't seem to run cold at any point, but eventually, I hear a little knock on the door and then Leo enters the bathroom. There's a door on the shower. He can't see in.

"Are you okay?"

"Yes."

"You've been in here a long time."

"I'm sorry." I shut the water off. "I don't want to make your bill too high."

"You won't," he says. He's still standing out there. He's not trying to sneak a peek at me or anything, so I'm not sure why he's still here. "Do you need help?"

"Help?"

"Because of..."

Because of my leg.

I don't really need his help. I can manage to get out of here, get my prosthetic back on, go to the bed, climb up on it, and then remove my leg for the night. I don't want to sleep with it on. It's not that I can't, it's just that it's not super comfortable, and sometimes it's nice to feel normal just for a little while.

Only...

Suddenly, that feels like so much work.

And he's *here*.

And he's *big*.

And it will be easy for him to carry me.

"Leo?"

"Yes?"

"Can you...can you carry me to the bed?"

I shouldn't be asking him, but I'm suddenly so very tired.

"I can carry you," he says.

I look down at myself. I'm naked. I know that he's going to like the way that I look. Curves and rolls and jiggles aren't going to matter to this alien man. He's not going to care.

Still, I appreciate it when he opens the door and hands me a little robe.

"Put this on. Tell me when you're ready."

A moment later, I tell him I'm ready, and he opens the door again.

"Do you want your glasses now?"

"No, I'll leave them in here."

There's nothing happening tonight that I need glasses for.

To my surprise, he hands me a bonnet.

"What is this?"

He blinks.

"It's a bonnet."

I know what a bonnet is. I just don't know why he has one. I've been wearing a bonnet for my hair for...my entire life.

I just didn't expect that my alien groom would just *happen* to have something for Black-girl hair in his house.

What the hell is happening?

"I know," I say slowly. "How do you have this?"

"Should I not? I've offended you." His eyes fall. "My brothers' wives told me that I need to have this on hand for my bride."

I reach for his arm, placing my hand gently on it.

"It's perfect," I tell him. "Thank you."

I slip the bonnet on and tuck my hair inside. Then I hold my arms out.

"Take me to bed, Leo. Take me to bed."

Chapter 12

Leo

I carry her to the bed and use one hand to pull back the covers of the bed. Then I gently place her down in the center and pull the blankets back up, tucking them around her. Tamara is silent the entire time.

Just as I'm about to get up and leave the room, she reaches for my arm and touches me. There's a slight hesitation there.

Is she nervous?

About me?

I don't want her to be nervous about me.

"Leo?"

"Yes, Tamara?"

"Are you...are you not interested in me?"

The question comes seemingly out of nowhere, and I shake my head.

"It's not that."

How am I supposed to tell her I've never done this before?

I really should have come up with a plan for this. I definitely should have talked to Miss Arieh about the entire I'm-a-virgin-with-no-tail thing, but I didn't, and now I'm kicking myself for it.

There's a part of me that wonders how this conversation is going to go because I don't want to tell her, but I also don't want her to worry because right now, Tamara looks like she wants to be devoured.

"I've never done this," I blurt out.

"Gotten married? Yeah, me neither," she sighs and shakes her head. "It's harder than it seems. Right? Like, I kind of thought I'd wear a big fluffy white dress and have all of my besties there."

I stare at her. "A white dress?"

"Earth custom," she shrugs.

"I'm sorry your...besties...weren't there."

She looks sad for a moment, lost in thought, but then she shrugs.

"What can you do? Life happens. Right?"

"Yeah," I nod.

Life happens. Only, I want more of it to happen and I want it to happen between us. I want to touch her and tease her and fall apart with her because she's absolutely, totally, insanely gorgeous.

And fun.

And curious.

Still, I can't tell her the truth just yet, so instead of climbing into bed with my new bride, and instead of offering her comfort, and instead of just sucking it up and telling her that I am, in fact, a first-time lover, I allow her to think that I've simply never been married and that I need some time to get used to the idea.

"Good night, Tamara," I tell her.

Then I turn and leave the room. Three cats follow me as I make my way back to the living room couch. This one hovers just above the ground. The nice thing about floating furniture is that it can easily be adjusted in height. If I need it higher, it can be higher. If I want it to rest on the floor, it can.

Right now, I like the way it floats just a few feet from the ground, and I climb on it, sprawling out on my back, and close my eyes.

I pretend that I'm in the ocean. I pretend I'm part of the sea and the waves are carrying me away. I pretend that the world isn't as scary as I've managed to make it be.

And then I fall asleep.

Chapter 13

Tamara

A virgin.

He's a hot, sexy virgin.

No, he's a hot, sexy *alien* virgin.

He's a virgin who got me a bonnet because he knows it helps me protect my hair. He's a virgin who took me to a bracelet shop and let me choose the most beautiful wedding band. And he's a virgin who is going to get me a kitten tomorrow because it's Grimalkin tradition and he gave the original kitten away to his cousin – the cousin who also stole his original bride.

And he's a virgin.

I keep my eyes closed as I think about what just went down between the two of us. There's no mistaking the fact that Leo was trying to be honest with me. He was obviously trying to tell me that he's never done *this*, meaning sex.

He's never had a woman gliding over him, sinking deep onto his length. He's never had someone losing her mind with pleasure while riding him.

He's never come with a girl before.

And I can be that girl.

I really wish Holly and Amena were here because they'd definitely know what to do. I can just picture Holly telling me to "slut it up" and Amena laughing and helping me choose just the right outfit.

Well, I don't have a lot of choices.

I don't *have* any outfits. I don't have anything sexy I can wear to make this really special for him.

And I really don't have easy access to my prosthetic because I left it in the bathroom.

Reaching to the sides of the walls, I run my hands until I find a couple of buttons. The first one I press raises the bed up. The second one lowers it back down. The third one turns the lights on.

And there's my leg.

It's right beside me in the bed and I didn't even notice.

He brought me my damn leg because that's the kind of guy he is.

Leo is the kind of man who is gentle and gracious and comforting.

He's the kind of guy who is going to make sure I have everything I need to feel safe and at home because he cares about me.

A lot.

More than he should.

He's going to be hurt when he finds out I'm leaving. It's going to kill him. I can already tell. I don't know a lot about Leo, but I know that he's the kind of person who actually gives a damn about the people around him who interact with him, so I know it's going to just destroy him when he realizes that I'm only here to find my friends.

And there's a part of me that feels really, really bad about this.

There's a part of me that feels like I'm somehow betraying him even though the two of us have only just met.

Because you married him, dumbass.

Before I can get too down on myself and before I can overthink this, reach for my prosthetic. I'm going to go to him. I'm going to go to him and I'm going to seduce him and I'm going to make this the best first time any guy has ever had because he deserves this.

He deserves this.

Chapter 14

Leo

I'm almost asleep when Erin starts purring. The black and white cat sleeping on my belly snuggles closer and sprawls out on my stomach.

Yes, she's a damn good cat.

They all are.

Erin suddenly jumps up and scurries away, and I lie there thinking about Tamara.

Why wasn't I just honest?

I should have been.

I should have just told her.

In fact, it's not really like me to wimp out like that.

I sit up, swinging my legs off the side of the couch. I don't need to be sleeping out here. Even if I go tell Tamara the truth, and even if I explain that I'm a tailless virgin and she's suddenly completely uninterested in me, then at least I'll know I was honest.

At least I'll be able to move forward with her knowing that I was real and that I shared.

So, I stand, ready to make my way to the bedroom. It's dark, and while I can see perfectly well in the darkness, I'm still careful to avoid stepping on the cats who keep scurrying silently around the house.

Do I have too many cats?

It's a question I think about sometimes, but no, I think I'm good. My brother Torao would tell me that there's no such thing as too many cats, and I'm honestly a bit inclined to agree with the man.

Is he generally an idiot?

Oh, yes.

Is he also generally correct?

Also, yes.

Stepping toward the room, I place my hand on the little panel to the side of the bedroom door so that it slides up and open. Then, without looking, I take a step into the room just as my sweet bride is taking a step out of the room. I didn't realize she was standing right there, which means that the two of us bump into each other wildly.

Before she can fall or stumble, I grab her, pulling her to myself, but then *I* stumble, barely missing stepping on Erin's tail, and the two of us go falling backward.

I groan as I land on my back in the living room with soft, sweet Tamara on top of me.

"Leo? I'm so sorry! I didn't even know you were up. I thought you were on the couch, and I was going to come find you and...oh..."

She's wiggling around on top of me, and yeah, my body is reacting to this. It's like the most wonderful, incredible feeling in the world, and I wish I'd been doing this with her the entire time instead of trying to hide and sleep on the couch like some schmuck.

"I'm sorry," I tell her.

She places both of her hands on my chest and shakes her head.

"I'm not."

"You're not?"

"No. Leo, I came to talk to you."

About what? Is she scared? Thirsty? Hungry? Does she need something else that I haven't provided for her? I start to feel a little bad, all of a sudden, but I think she realizes that there's a bunch of chaos reigning in my head because she presses her lips to mine, all of a sudden, and my head completely clears.

Now, the only thing I'm thinking about is her.

Right now, the only thing that matters is her.

All of her.

All of Tamara.

Chapter 15

Tamara

There's no logical reason this make out session should feel as good as it does, yet here we are. I'm on top of him on the floor of his house. There are probably cats running all around, but the only thing I care about is getting closer to him.

Kissing him.

Falling for him.

It's been less than a day since I landed on Grimalkin and I'm already losing my mind over this guy.

"Tamara," he finally pulls back. "Are you okay?"

"I know you meant," I say. I'm not going to play coy with him.

"You...you know?"

"I know you're a virgin," I say.

He looks a little squeamish at the word, but he doesn't hurry up and leave or anything like that. Instead, he waits.

"Why?" It's probably a rude question, but I do want to know.

This man is handsome. He's a doctor. He's strong. He's bold. He's incredible.

So, why is it that he hasn't *been* with a woman?

Why hasn't he been with anyone in an intimate way?

Surely, he's dated. I can't believe that he's never dated. Then again, perhaps that's not really how things on Grimalkin are done. Maybe all Grimalkin men wait until they're ready to take a bride until they start being playful, but I somehow completely doubt that.

Leo looks at me. He's beneath me and his hands are on my hips. I'm not comfortable. My prosthetic is bending at sort of a weird angle. My hips ache. He seems to sense this because somehow, he manages to stand up while *holding* me and carries me into the bedroom. He sets me down and then he sits beside me.

"I was busy," he says.

"Busy?"

"I was in school and then university and then doing my medical training. I was focused. I was shy."

"That can't be it, though," I say quietly. "There must be more to it than that."

He shrugs. "Not everyone is especially outgoing when it comes to making love, Tamara. By the time I was working, it seemed like the time for losing my virginity had come and gone."

"You were worried people would think you were weird," I point out.

He nods.

"Do most Grimalkins date before they get married? Like, if you know you're going to arrange for a bride, do you still date people?"

"Some do. Some go to other planets. I'm quite sure both of my brothers had their first sexual experiences on Malum or Chaos. I know that Torao, at least, has slept with women on almost every planet. By the time he got married, he was quite experienced in lovemaking."

"Interesting. I bet he learned some weird stuff."

"He likes to have fun," Leo agrees. "There's something else, though. Something I should have told you before we got married."

He hesitates for a moment.

"You're already married," I whisper. "Is that it?"

"What? No! How would I be a virgin if I'm already married?"

"Alien men are sneaky," I shrug. Nothing would surprise me at this point.

"I'm not already married."

"Then you're not really from Grimalkin. Is that it? Is this entire bridal thing a sham?"

He stares, blinking.

"You're a serial killer. Is that it? Because I don't really feel like getting murdered just yet. I still have things I need to do with my life." You know, like finding my besties. Holly and Amena are here somewhere. I just have to figure out where.

Tomorrow, I'm going to find out if there's some sort of bridal hangout. I'm guessing that there's something for the brides to do while they're waiting on their darling husbands all of the time.

Leo has a job, as I'm sure most of the other Grimalkin men do, but not me.

With my absence of a second leg, I'm not even sure I'm going to be able to *get* a job. It depends on how discriminatory people here end up being. Well, that and how much I want to hide the truth about who I am.

"I'm not a serial killer," Leo says.

"Then what could be so terrible that you didn't want to tell me?"

He takes a deep breath.

"I'm not sure how to tell you this, so I'm just going to tell you. Tamara, I don't have a tail."

Chapter 16

Leo

Out of every possible reaction I could have imagined, I never thought that a huge grin covering her face would be the response I received.

"Did you just say that you don't have a tail?"

"Yes."

"Let me see."

"What? No," I shake my head.

"Oh, please," she says. She's grinning like a crazy woman and I'm not sure what I'm supposed to do.

"Why are you so excited? I thought you'd be upset."

"And I thought you were going to tell me you had a fake family or that you were planning to murder me. Come on, Leo," she smiles. She takes my hands, leans forward, and kisses me. "I'll get naked first," she says.

And that's when I realize what's really happening.

I'm imperfect.

I'm not the massive alien behemoth she planned to wed when she got here. I don't have a huge, flawless tail. I'm not as *pretty* as my brothers are.

I'm just...me.

And that's okay with her because that's what she needs.

She doesn't need someone who hits the gym constantly. She doesn't need a guy who is swimming in pools of money. She doesn't need someone who will fight off the wild cats of Grimalkin for her.

She just needs me.

And I'm going to be there for her.

"Come here," I murmur, and I grab her by the throat to tug her close to me. She groans as I kiss her – really kiss her.

Earlier, I was holding back, but now that I know she isn't scared of me, we're going to make this happen. The two of us *have* to make this happen because I need her more than I've ever needed anything.

There's a deep craving that's growing in me, but before we do this, before we take things to the next step, I want her to be comfortable.

"Wait," I pull away. "Shall we remove your leg?"

She blinks, staring at me. "What?"

I point to her prosthetic. I don't mind that she has it. It's actually pretty cool. Tamara has drawn all sorts of pictures on it with silver ink. The leg itself is dark brown and matches her pretty skin, but she's decorated the leg with stars and hearts and swirls.

"Will you be comfortable?" I ask.

"I don't usually take it off during sex," she admits. She looks away for a moment. "Most people don't want to talk about it."

I reach for her chin and turn her head back to mine.

"We don't have to talk about it," I tell her. I don't like talking about my lack of tail, after all. "I want you to feel comfortable, though. How would you like us to do this?"

I stare at her, and she shakes her head.

"What is it?"

"Why'd you have to be so wonderful?" Tamara whispers. "Why couldn't you have just been mean?"

Chapter 17

Tamara

He's not supposed to be like this.

He's not supposed to be caring and calm and kind and passionate.

He's supposed to be gruff and scary and mean.

"Can you give me a minute?" I ask him.

"Anything you need."

He kisses me again, and then he disappears into the other room. I sit there for a moment thinking about everything that's happened.

He really wants me to feel safe.

He wants me to feel comfortable and at ease and in control of everything I'm dealing with.

This is a guy who wants to make sure that at the end of the day, I feel like I'm empowered to do whatever it takes to find my own happiness.

This is a guy who believes in me.

And I'm...

I'm lying to him.

I'm only here to find my friends.

I can't fall for him.

I'm not supposed to.

I definitely didn't think I'd feel this attraction to him on the first day. I definitely didn't think I'd be falling for him in a matter of hours. This is the type of thing that happens to girls in books. It's *not* the type of thing that happens to me.

But if that's true, then why do I feel like I'm falling for him?

And why do I feel like I'm going to float away if he doesn't start kissing me again?

And why – oh why – do I feel like my heart can't take much more of this?

I'm just about to take off my bonnet and pull my leg off when he comes back into the room. Instantly, I know that something has changed. I don't know what, but there's a problem.

"Leo?"

"It's my brother. He just called. He runs a cat palace."

He's mentioned this brother before. From what I can tell, he's got two of them and all three of them seem quite close. I know that he has cousins, too, but beyond that, this man's life is a mystery.

"He needs my help. A cat is sick." Leo pauses, looking at me. "Would you like to come with me?"

He's inviting me to be part of his life. He isn't just letting me crash at his place while I figure out what I'm going to do with my life. He isn't just trying to get me to survive here.

He's trying to include me.

"Yes," I tell him. I'm a little nervous at the prospect of meeting his brother, but maybe it's a good thing. I need to remember why I'm actually here and stop allowing myself to get swept up in the romance of the moment.

Leo isn't mine.

He's not going to *be* mine.

I'd do well to remember that.

"Let's go," he says to me. "We need to hurry."

I nod, suddenly glad that I didn't actually take off my leg. Leo helps me down from the bed and rushes to grab some clothing from a drawer. He produces what looks like an oversized trench coat.

"Really?"

He looks down at the garment in his hand.

"Do you dislike it?"

I stare at him. It's better than what I'm currently wearing, which is the robe he gave me in the shower. I kept it on and will happily change it for the coat. Still, I need some real clothes.

"It's fine," I tell him. "But I need better clothing."

I'm saying this in what probably sounds like a mean way, but he nods.

"Of course," he agrees. "We will buy you something suitable tomorrow."

"Multiple suitable things," I clarify. "I need multiple outfits."

He reaches for me and pulls me into his arms. Then he kisses me in that passionate way only he manages to do.

"Of course," he says. "Whatever you need. Now get changed so we can go. My brother needs us."

Chapter 18

Leo

We arrive at Torao's place to find him sitting outside of the house he shares with Amena. He's sitting on the porch holding the kitten he called about.

"I don't think she's going to make it," he says as I hop out of the floating car and run to him.

"Let's get her inside," I say, and I guide my brother back into his house.

It's rare that Torao calls me. It's even rarer that he calls me in the middle of the night. I make it a point to come visit him and his animals at least once a week, but he doesn't usually have to deal with sick kittens.

Tamara follows closely as the three of us go back into Torao's home. There's a table in the center of the room that wasn't there before.

"New addition?" I ask, placing the little cat on it.

"I asked my wife to set it up while I was calling you," he explains. "Can you help her? Is it too late?"

He's panicking, which means it's my job to keep him calm. This is much easier said than done. I need him to relax so that I can focus on this kitten, who appears to be breathing with a lot of difficulty.

Somehow, Tamara seems to recognize this.

I don't know how she does it, but she manages to draw Torao's attention away from me and toward her.

"Excuse me," she says.

He looks at her like he's noticing her for the first time.

"Where did you come from?"

"I'm Tamara. Leo's wife."

"Leo's...wife?"

"We got married today. It's nice to meet you. You're his older brother, right?"

I glance up to see Torao nodding. His eyes are still on me, but I nod at him, and he turns back to my wife. Good. He needs to focus on something while I figure out what's going on with this kitten.

I had planned on bringing Tamara here tomorrow so she could choose her bridal kitten. It's a bit unconventional, really, letting a bride choose her own kitten.

Then again, there's not really anything conventional at all about the way our relationship has unfolded.

I'm almost completely sure that she sneaked onto the ship that was coming here, and I don't know why.

I don't *need* to know why, but I can make a couple of educated guesses.

I'm not an idiot.

I know that Holly, Ekpen's wife, came to Grimalkin because Earth has been falling apart for a long time and it's only gotten worse and worse. I know that Amena came to save her. I know that Amena doesn't really have anything holding her to Earth anymore, so she felt like she could come here and have everything work out.

But Tamara?

Well, Tamara is a mystery to me.

If she's following in Holly's footsteps, it's possible that she just wanted a nice escape. Maybe she thought marrying a nice alien man would be an upgrade from the life she was living.

Or perhaps she knows a bridal candidate who came to Grimalkin and was chosen to stay. That's another very real possibility.

There are so many possible reasons, but it only took her one.

Just one reason.

And now she's here.

She's here and I can't let our wedding night end in a kitten dying.

I can't let this be her introduction to the planet.

So, I turn back to the little creature, and I make it a promise.

"I won't let you die."

Chapter 19

Tamara

We both hear him say it.

We both hear him promise the little cat that it's not going to die, and there's a part of my heart that feels like it's just breaking in two in that moment.

Torao steps away from Leo and moves to stand beside me.

"Let's leave him here," he murmurs, and something tells me that Torao has been down this road with Leo before and that he understands what his brother actually needs.

Not me.

I don't know what he needs because I barely know the man. I don't know what he needs because the two of us aren't actually close. I don't know what he needs because we're practically strangers who met only this morning, but...

But I like him.

And I hate that I feel this way.

This entire journey was supposed to be simple and easy. I was supposed to come here and slink around the planet until I found my friends. Maybe I'd die trying, but it didn't matter because I know they've always got my back.

Only, it kind of does matter, doesn't it?

I allow myself to be led from the house and back out to the front. Torao gestures to the front step and I sit down. He drops besides me. He's big and bulky, like Leo, but there's no attraction there. I do notice the way Torao's tail swishes behind him. I don't know how to read Grimalkin body language, though, so I don't know if he's angry or sad or being sneaky or what.

"Why are you here?" Torao asks.

I stiffen, unhappy with the question. He's blunt and to the point, and I don't like it. I don't answer right away, but he presses.

"Tell me why you've married my brother."

"He was assigned to me as my husband when I landed on Grimalkin."

At least that much is true.

The two of us were chosen to be mates by Miss Arieh. Yes, there was another woman who was originally chosen for him, but even matchmakers can screw up sometimes.

Right?

Besides, if I wasn't worried about locating my friends, I'd be a little more likely to allow myself to get swept up in Leo's advances.

I've already looked at my communications unit I was given earlier. There's nothing on it that offers me any sort of hope of finding my friends. I'd really started to believe that I'd be able to come here and just find them, but...

Well, that hasn't happened.

"There's more to it, isn't there?" Torao asks. Not a lot gets by him. I think that comes from being the middle child. My grandma was a middle child and she always told me that her older sister didn't tell her things because she was private, and her younger brother didn't tell her things because he was sneaky. It was always up to my grandma to just observe people and try to figure things out on her own.

"No," I lie. "There's nothing more to it than that."

Torao considers this. He's not calling me out just yet, but he does spend an awful lot of time staring at me.

I'm worried about Holly and Amena. I'm worried that they're trapped somewhere or that they're having terrible marriages. Not every Grimalkin can be as nice as Leo.

Right?

Torao looks away from me. He's staring up at the sky. Grimalkin is a planet with multiple moons and a whole lot of stars. It's almost as bright at night as it is during the day, at least out here at Torao's place. Maybe it feels different in the city.

"He's a good man," Torao says.

"I know."

"I don't think that you do. He's a good man, and he doesn't deserve to be hurt."

I turn to gawk at Torao. Is he *really* giving me the big-brother speech?

"I'm not going to hurt him."

"You'd better not," he says. Torao stands and stares down at me. "If you hurt my brother, I'll kill you."

Then he goes back inside, and I'm left wondering what the hell I'm going to do.

Chapter 20

Leo

Torao comes back in the main floor of his home just as I'm placing the kitten in a little box.

"She's dead," he says, his voice flat, as though he can't summon up any more energy.

"What? No!" I say hastily, looking down at the little cat. "She's totally fine. She just needed medication. She was having trouble breathing."

"Asthmatic kitty, huh?"

"Something like that."

Sometimes kittens come from off-planet and have breathing troubles on Grimalkin. It's kind of a weird situation, actually. The air is different here, and not every cat is compatible. This one will be just fine, but she recently arrived from Sapphira. She just needs a little bit of time.

"Thank you, brother," Torao says, clapping a hand on my shoulder.

"It was nothing."

A few of his other cats have wandered down from the second floor using the little platforms he and Ekpen love so much. There are always cats going up and coming down. It's quite overwhelming, in my experience.

This main floor is usually pretty empty, and I suspect that as soon as I leave, Torao will put the table away and take this kitten back to the other cats from Sapphira. He keeps some of the cats in the main house, but he also has spaces outside and in his outbuilding - which kind of resembles an Earth barn.

"I'd like to keep the kitten," I tell him. It's going to be the perfect little cat for Tamara. Even though I assumed I'd let her choose the cat she wants, I think this one really will be perfect.

"Are you sure?"

"I'm sure. The cat will be fine. She just needs a name." Tamara will be able to choose something lovely for her.

"About Tamara," Torao says.

I look at my brother and raise an eyebrow. I don't have to ask him what the hell he's talking about because it's written all over his face.

"There's something about her," he says. "I can't quite put my finger on it, but there's something you don't know."

I know what he means because I've had the same feeling. I still don't really know why Tamara came to Grimalkin. She gave me a vague sort of answer about wanting a fresh start, but that can't be the only reason.

Someone who wants a fresh start could go anywhere.

Why her?

Why here?

I can't worry about it now, though, because I need to go get cleaned up. The kitten is sleeping in the little box, which I set back down on the table. I slip my communications wristlet off and set it down, rubbing my wrist. I'm sweaty and tired and all I want to do is go back home and climb back into bed with Tamara.

"Where is she?" I ask.

"She's still outside."

I nod. I'm ready to leave, but I need to go wash up first. I'm covered in random germs and gunk from taking care of the kitty.

"I need to go wash my hands," I tell my brother.

"I'll come with you."

"Are you so scared of being alone with my bride that you're going to try to ride up on the platform with me?" I chuckle. We both know the platforms that move to the next floor are made for exactly one person.

Torao is quiet as comes up next to me.

"We won't both fit."

He glares at me as he climbs on the platform first and then grabs me around the legs and lifts me up so he's holding me.

"What the hell are you doing?" I ask.

"You're not leaving me down here," he chuckles. Then the platform starts moving up, and I hold perfectly still as we go to the next floor. I'm going to hurry so that Tamara and I can get going. The cat is okay, and I'm okay, and Torao is okay. Well, aside from being a little weird. We reach the next floor of his house and I manage to escape from his hold and land on my feet. He steps off the platform, too.

Amena, his wife, is here yawning.

"Hey boys," she says. "Coffee?"

One thing I've learned in the months since my brothers got married is that humans love coffee. Whether they're tired or sad or hungry or happy, they always seem to want coffee. I make a mental note to find some for Tamara so she can be happy, too.

"No," I tell her. I still can't stomach the beverage, but I'm glad it makes her happy.

"Is the kitty okay?" Amena asks, moving to Torao. She presses her hands on his chest and smiles up at him. My brother grins.

"She's going to be just fine, thanks to Leo."

Chapter 21

Tamara

I sit outside for a long time. Two little white cats come over to me and start purring. I pet them happily, content at the moment to have someone with me.

I finally get up and head back inside. The main room on this floor is strangely empty aside from the table and a little box on top of it.

"Hello?" I offer quietly. I'm not sure where Torao and Leo have gone. The space feels strangely empty and quiet without them in it, but I'm not really sure what I'm supposed to do now.

Where are the stairs?

The doors?

Grimalkin is a strange place. I know that Miss Arieh would run little patterns on the walls with her hands. Those patterns would cause the walls to move up and down as she needed them to, but I don't know if that's how Torao's house works.

Annoyed and tired, I walk over to the table in the center of the room. I can just sit down next to it and wait. Eventually, Leo will have to come back for me.

Right?

I don't think he's left me here. He must be around here somewhere, although I'm not sure where. I glance up at the ceiling and notice there are a couple of little round spots where the ceiling doesn't quite match.

Are those entrances to the next floors?

Platform lifts, maybe?

I don't know.

Looking at the table in front of me, which is the only damn thing in this room, I look at the little box. There's a tiny blue kitten inside who appears to be sleeping. She's okay, I realize. Leo has worked his magic and she's okay.

"Fluffy," I say quietly, petting her. I know instantly that *Fluffy* is the perfect name for this particular cat. She's soft and sweet and she starts purring right away, and I know that I need her.

Will they let me have her?

The kitten's eyes flutter open for just a moment as she looks at me, and I get the feeling that she rather likes her new name. This makes me even happier.

Then I feel a little vibration.

She's not purring, though. It's the communications device next to the box.

It's Leo's.

He's taken off his watch and set it here, and I reach for it instantly.

Why would he take this off?

Is he okay?

Instantly, my heart begins to worry as I realize that Leo might actually be in trouble. How much does he *really* know about this brother of his, after all? It's not like this would have been the first time someone had been betrayed by their brother.

I flick on the communications watch. Maybe if I call Torao, I can find Leo and figure out where he's gone and what's happened. If Torao has betrayed Leo and actually captured him or sneaked him out of here somehow, I want to know.

Maybe I can't find my friends or save them, but there must be a chance for me to save Leo.

I like this man.

A lot.

This is the kind of man who prepared a bonnet for me. He might not have gotten an assortment of clothing ready, but he had a damn bonnet. He helped me to the bed. He didn't give a damn that I don't have both of my legs anymore. He didn't care.

He just...

He's compassionate in all things and at all times.

He's incredible.

A holographic menu appears, and I navigate through it until I find Torao's contact information. He's listed as TORAO – BROTHER as though there are multiple people named Torao on Grimalkin, which I simply don't believe.

I press a button to call, and a moment later, Torao's face appears in holographic form in front of me.

"Tamara?"

Torao looks confused.

Really confused.

"Do you have him, you son of a bitch?"

Okay, so I'm not staying calm at all.

"What?"

"You'd better let him go, Torao. All that talk about how you'd kill me if I hurt him and now you're the one hurting him. Let him go."

Suddenly, I'm completely overwhelmed. I know that I'm not much of a fighter. I'm not strong. I'm not nimble. I can't move very quickly, and I certainly can't take down a giant alien, but the more I think about it, the more concerned I am that he's got my man.

Why else would Leo have left his communications wristlet?

Why else would he have left the kitten he just fought to save?

It all makes sense in some weird, twisted sort of way. Torao called Leo in the middle of the night. He didn't know I'd be coming to throw a wrench in his plans. All he knew was that he'd be able to get his brother here quickly and discreetly so he could – what? Kill him? Maybe there's some inheritance money or something equally nefarious.

But I need him.

I've only known Leo for hours, and I *need* him.

"Where the fuck is he?" I scream out.

"Tamara," Torao speaks in that deep Grimalkin voice of his. He's obviously trying to stay calm because I'm screaming at him, but I know that whatever he says is just going to piss me off more. "I didn't hurt my brother."

"Then where is he?"

Where could he possibly fucking be?

I don't know where they could have gone or why they sneaked past me. There are other floors in this building that I can't access because I don't know how. They've disappeared and once again, I'm all alone.

But then I feel two strong hands on my shoulders, and I turn around.

"I'm right here," Leo says.

I look up at the ceiling, and sure enough, there's an open circle there. He must have ridden some kind of platform down to the first floor.

"You aren't hurt," I whisper.

"I'm not hurt."

"I thought he abducted you."

It sounds so stupid to say out loud.

"And you were worried." Leo has the audacity to smile a little bit at this realization.

"Hey," I slap him playfully. "That's not okay to tease me."

I actually was worried, and I probably owe Torao an apology. I kiss Leo on the cheek before turning back to the holographic call.

That's when I hear a familiar voice.

"Torao, what the hell? Is that Tamara?"

It's Amena.

She's here.

Chapter 22

Leo

WE ALL FIND OURSELVES settled in Torao's living room with Ekpen and Holly, whom we've called over. Apparently, our brides were all best friends back on Earth and because the communications devices that Holly and Amena smuggled in didn't work correctly – or, in Holly's case, were eaten by a lumao – Tamara thought they'd been captured.

Only, they'd had their hearts captured by love.

Holly is pregnant and I'm quite sure that Amena is, too, even though she hasn't announced it yet. I glance over at Tamara and wonder if she's going to want to stay with me now that she's found her friends. I realize now that this is her real motive for coming to Grimalkin.

She needed to make sure that they're okay.

"I can't believe you're really here," Holly says, holding Tamara's hands.

"It's insane," Amena agrees.

It's the middle of the night and my brothers and I feel exhausted, but the women are wildly awake and ready to talk. They have so much catching up to do – talking about life on

Grimalkin, warning each other about the predatory cats that lurk in the hillsides, and catching up on what it's like to finally be married.

I sit, watching them drink their coffee and share their stories, and I wonder how I managed to get so lucky to find Tamara.

"What happened?" Torao asks me. He's sitting with me and Ekpen at the back of the room. We're giving the women some space as they explore together, talking and sharing. It warms my heart to see them so happy.

I only wish Tamara had told me sooner that she was worried about her friends.

I could have helped her out and given her a little bit of peace. I could have offered her the knowledge that everyone here is fine. They're all safe. Grimalkin just sort of *sucks* – to use a word Holly recently taught me – when it comes to communicating with Earth.

"Apollo took the woman I was supposed to marry," I tell them. "Kate." She's a pretty lady – luscious and curvy – but she was never for me. Miss Arieh made a mistake in matching us. Something tells me she was always meant to be Apollo's.

"Sounds like something Apollo would do," Torao grumbles.

"He is the worst," Ekpen agrees.

"He's not the worst." He just wants someone. Needs someone.

"All right," Ekpen concedes. "Perhaps he's not as troublesome as his brothers are, but as a group..." He shakes his head and I just bite back a laugh.

"That's our cousin, for you."

I hope he finds his happiness, though, just as my own brothers and I are finding happiness.

We stay until the sun begins to rise, and then I take Tamara and Fluffy, her new kitten, back to our house. We find Fluffy a safe little spot to sleep – a little bed at the foot of our own – and then Tamara and I climb into bed together.

"Let's try this again," I laugh, kissing her and pulling her tight. She kisses me back eagerly before pulling away.

"I need a minute," she says. I know she wants to take her prosthetic off and get comfortable, but I also don't want her to feel like this is something she needs to hide or something she needs to worry about.

"Would you..." I think about how I should ask this, but I decide that being blunt is the best option. "Would you like me to help you?"

I want to. I want to learn everything I need to know about taking care of Tamara. She's sweet, and she's soft, and she's so damn perfect in every way.

"You want to help me?" Tamara asks, raising an eyebrow.

I nod. "Of course. You're my wife."

"You know," she looks away for a moment before turning back, "I've never had anyone offer, and I appreciate that." She bites her lip. "I'm not ready for that yet, Leo. I don't know if this is something I'll ever want your help with, but I appreciate knowing you want to be involved in caring for me."

"That's okay," I kiss her. "I'll wait right outside and I'll come back when you're ready. Okay?"

She nods, and I go to the door and step outside.

Chapter 23

Tamara

This has been one hell of a day.

My prosthetic leg is something I've had to deal with my entire life. It's something that's always impacted me and my ability to be mobile, but it's never been something I've shared with another person. And while I think Leo's offer to help me take it off and get ready for *whatever* it is that the two of us are going to do is kind of sweet and honestly, a little bit of a turn-on, it's not something I want him to help me with.

I've never wanted help.

Even as a kid when my grandmother wanted to help me, I always preferred doing things myself or working with a nurse. It's just a very personal thing, and even though I am married to Leo, and even though I think I'd like to stay here and stay married to him, I'm not ready for that.

Luckily, he seems okay with it.

Once my prosthesis is off and set carefully to the side, I sit on the bed for a moment.

There are so many different emotions going through my head but all of them center on the idea that I think I'm supposed to be here.

I think I'm supposed to be here with Leo.

I think I'm supposed to be falling in love with this guy, and I'm not sure why I'm so sure about this except that for the first time in a very long time, everything feels right.

I was nothing more than a stowaway who managed to get lucky and now I'm about to climb into bed with a guy who makes me feel like I'm worth more than anything else.

"Leo?" I call out awkwardly. It's been a while since I was with someone new, but I've *never* been with someone like Leo.

He's *big*.

And green.

And when he comes back into the room, he looks nervous and excited and luscious as hell.

Oh, yeah.

This is right where I'm supposed to be.

And I'm the experienced one, so I'm not afraid to be a little bossy.

I'm sitting on the bed wearing the long coat he gave me earlier. I unbutton it slowly as he stands in the doorway watching me. I like the idea of giving him a show. I like the idea of him getting turned on while he watches me because I can already see just how into me he is.

He's hard.

His length is pressing against the front of his black pants, trying to get out, and I don't think I've ever wanted anything as much as I want him right now.

"You look beautiful," he tells me.

I smile as I finish unbuttoning the jacket and pushing it back. It falls off my shoulders and then it's just me. I'm naked here before him and I'm just *me*.

I've got curves and rolls and scars. I've got boobs that sag just a little. They aren't tight and perky and tiny. I've only got one leg.

But he doesn't care about the things I view as imperfections.

He's looking at me like he wants to devour me and suddenly, that's exactly what I want.

"Come here," I whisper, beckoning him to me, and he makes his way to the bed. I know that he's never done *this* before, but I also know that he's probably done *stuff*.

He steps in front of me and I slip my leg around him, tugging him closer. My hands grab his ass as he leans down and kisses me. He might be new to sex, but he's not afraid to dominate my mouth. He's not afraid to take control in this moment.

But soon it's my turn.

"I'm naked," I say.

"I'm well aware." He grins. "You look fucking incredible. Look at these gorgeous tits," he murmurs, bouncing one of my breasts just a little before he starts twirling one of his thumbs over my nipple. "Fucking lovely."

Lovely.

He thinks I'm lovely.

"I want to see you, too," I whisper.

He grins. "You should have told me so sooner," he laughs, and he pulls his shirt off. I know that Leo is a little nervous about being naked with me because he doesn't have a tail the way his brothers do, but I don't care about that.

I care about the fact that this big green alien in front of me is covered with the sexiest-looking scales I've ever seen in my life.

"Leo, you've been holding back on me," I look up at him. "You should have been shirtless all day."

He smirks. "Is that what you like? Baby, I don't know if my patients are going to like me going into work without any clothes on."

"Trust me," I whisper. "It doesn't matter if your patients are people or pets, they're going to love these."

I reach out, running my palms over his hard scales. He groans a little, enjoying the sensation just as much as I'm enjoying giving it to him. I love making him feel like this. I love making him feel like he's going to fall apart because that's what he's doing to *me*.

He's making *me* feel like I'm going to die if he doesn't get inside of me, and this is a feeling I've been craving for a very long time.

He climbs up onto the bed with me, kissing me and teasing my body. He finally ends up taking his pants off and I wrap my hand firmly around his long, green cock, stroking him as he plays with my breasts.

Leo's taking his time, and I like that.

When he slides a hand down my tummy and to my pussy, it doesn't take long before I'm on the verge of coming for him. This entire day has been one rollercoaster of emotions after another, and I'm so excited that I can't hold back.

I don't want to hold back.

And he knows.

"Come for me," he murmurs. "You beautiful human. Let me feel you."

"Tell me again," I whisper.

"I need you. I need you to come for me, baby. Come for me, Tamara."

It's like my heart and my body explode at the same time. I shouldn't feel as safe and as comfortable with him as I do. He lets me be myself and he doesn't care that I don't match what the other girls look like.

He just likes me.

He snuggles close to me, rubbing his cheek against mine.

"That was so perfect," he murmurs.

"I want more," I tell him.

"Tell me what you want, Tamara. I'll give you anything."

I reach for him, stroking him.

"I want this. I want your cock."

"How do you want me?" Leo grins.

It can be a little awkward to find a position that I'm comfortable in, but there are a few that have worked well for me in the past, and I motion for him to climb over me. I lie down on my back with a few pillows beneath my head and shoulders, and he settles over me. His cock nudges at my entrance, but thanks to a damn day of foreplay, I'm already wet and ready for him.

"Are you sure?" Leo whispers. "We don't have to if you aren't ready."

"I'm sure," I tell him.

I'm sure.

When he slides inside of me, filling me, the look that comes over his face is pure satisfaction. This might be his first time, but he knows what he's doing. He lowers his head and kisses me as he slides in and out of me, filling me over and over again.

He's letting me know in this moment just what he thinks of me, and I know perfectly well what I think of him.

He's perfect.

Tail or no tail, he's everything I could have hoped for in a groom, and I don't know how I got so damn lucky to have been matched with him, especially randomly.

He props himself up with his hands on either side of my head as he thrusts deeper and deeper. I know that he's getting close and I reach around to his back and start running my nails down his skin.

It's his turn to come for me.

It's his turn to fill me up with his seed.

He groans as he comes, thrusting deep into me one last time, but then something else happens. As he lowers his body back down, bringing his face to mine once more, I realize that my new husband is *purring*.

Chapter 24

Leo

A few months later

"I'm pregnant," Tamara says, smiling at my brothers and their wives. She's pregnant with a little Grimalkin baby who is going to look much cuter than the one currently resting in Ekpen's arms. He and Holly have an absolute *glow* about them that's kind of annoying, but everyone is happy – including my parents, who finally have the chance to spoil grandchildren.

Fluffy is purring in Tamara's arms as everyone gathers around her to congratulate her. She's thrilled, and honestly, so I am. Hopefully our babies take after her and not me because she's damn gorgeous. In fact, she's the prettiest thing I've ever seen in my life, and I don't know how I got so lucky as to fall for her.

If Miss Arieh hadn't made a mistake and tried to match me with Kate, and if my damn cousin hadn't interjected and stolen her away, I might never have had the chance to meet the one person I'm supposed to be with.

Tamara is patient and kind and good with animals, and she's taken a job working for Torao at his cat palace, which is a lot of fun. She loves getting to spend time with the animals and Fluffy enjoys getting to go to work with her every day.

"I'm thrilled," Callie, my mother, says.

"You're going to be wonderful parents," my dad agrees.

Holly and Amena both start talking at once and congratulating Tamara. My brothers both look at me and wink. They know that the reason we all take brides from Earth is to repopulate Grimalkin, which means that every new baby is celebrated wildly. They also know that the three of us have been damn lucky to have been matched with such wonderful, incredible brides.

We've all been blessed beyond measure to have had the chance to fall in love.

Until Tamara walked into my life, I hadn't known just how fantastic having a human bride really could be. Having someone who accepts me in spite of all of my mistakes and who adores me even when I screw up is really...

Well, there are no words.

Except joy.

I'm content.

I'm in love.

We're all happy here today.

Except, apparently, Apollo.

We all turn in unison as the door to my parents' house flies up. Apollo knows the code to enter the house and apparently none of us noticed him using it. Now he's standing soaking wet in the doorway. Rain is pouring into the house and seeping into my mother's carpet, but we barely notice because we're staring at Apollo.

The dude looks absolutely, totally, completely miserable. I've never seen anyone looking as unhappy as him. Then again, the last time I saw him was on his wedding day, which is also my wedding day.

"Apollo?" I ask, taking a step toward him. "Cousin, are you all right?"

"What's the matter?" Ekpen asks. He and Torao come with me as we step toward Apollo. Everyone else stays where they are – Tamara with her kitten, Holly with her baby, and Mom, Dad, and Amena standing close to Tamara.

"What's the matter?" Apollo spits out. "What's the matter?" He shakes his head and holds his arms out. "What's the *matter* is that *she's* gone." He glares at me and points. "And it's all your fault."

⧌⧌⧌

THE END

Want more of Grimalkin?

Want to find out what happens to Apollo and Kate?

<u>Find out in ALIEN INDULGENCE (Grimalkin Beasts Book 1).</u>[1]

If you're looking for more sci-fi books by Sophie Stern, check out her standalones:

Alien Dragon

Alien Beast

Alien Monster

Alien Conquest

You can also dive into a sci-fi series like:

The Hidden Planet Trilogy

Aliens of Malum series

---

1. *https://books2read.com/u/4jqGVl*

Alien Chaos series
In the Darkness
All of Sophie's sci-fi books take place in the same universe, so you can jump from book to book easily!

Author

Sophie Stern writes bad boys and feisty heroines. Her work ranges from contemporary to science fiction to paranormal and everything in-between. This is her first book in the Intergalactic Dating Agency, but it certainly won't be her last. Sophie loves writing aliens because there's nothing quite like traveling to a new place and experiencing a whole new world, especially when the people you meet are unlike anything you could have possibly imagined.

Follow her on Facebook for frequent updates or check her out on TikTok for teasers of her latest stories.

Thank you so much for reading!

Intergalactic Dating Agency

Looking for more out of this world romance?

Your local Intergalactic Dating Agency can help!

These strong, smart, sexy aliens are on the prowl for mates, and humans like you are exactly what they're after. Jump in with Book 1 of any standalone trilogy from our crew of rock star SFR authors and make steamy first contact!

Warning: abductions may or may not be included!

Grab more hunky alien action here:

http://romancingthealien.com[1]

---

1.   http://romancingthealien.com/?fbclid=IwAR1MEzgBbv8HnYfFzebULIzTwY7
K6z-zo7BhxfFixvzPvcmEwK9sBGfvYWA

Don't miss out!

Visit the website below and you can sign up to receive emails whenever Sophie Stern publishes a new book. There's no charge and no obligation.

https://books2read.com/r/B-A-XOYC-ICZBC

BOOKS 2 READ

Connecting independent readers to independent writers.

Did you love *Leo (Intergalactic Dating Agency)*? Then you should read *Alien Dragon*[2] by Sophie Stern!

I'm on the last ship out. I don't think I'm going to make it, but I do. Earth is dying and there's only one way I can possibly survive: fight for a spot on the dragon planet of Taneyemm. They don't want humans there. They don't like us. They don't know us. But when I step foot on the ship bound for Taneyemm, I know it's my last hope. I'll do anything I have to survive. I'll do whatever it takes. When I finally reach my destination and I see the alien dragons for the first time, I realize

---

2. https://books2read.com/u/bzParG

3. https://books2read.com/u/bzParG

I'm in way over my head. And I don't know if my heart is ready for this.

Also by Sophie Stern

Alien Chaos
Destroyed
Guarded
Saved
Christmas on Chaos
Alien Chaos: A Sci-Fi Alien Romance Bundle

Aliens of Malum
Deceived: An Alien Brides Romance
Betrayed: An Alien Brides Romance
Fallen: An Alien Brides Romance
Captured: An Alien Brides Romance
Regret
Crazed
For Keeps
Rotten: An Alien Brides Romance

Anchored
Starboard
Battleship
All Aboard
Abandon Ship
Below Deck
Crossing the Line
Anchored: Books 1-3
Anchored: Books 4-6

Ashton Sweets
Christmas Sugar Rush
Valentine's Sugar Rush
St. Patty's Sugar Rush
Halloween Sugar Rush

Bullies of Crescent Academy
You Suck
Troublemaker
Jaded

Club Kitten Dancers
Move

Pose
Climb

Dragon Enchanted
Hidden Mage
Hidden Captive
Hidden Curse

Fate High School
You Wish: A High School Reverse Harem Romance
Freak: A Reverse Harem High School Romance
Get Lost: A Reverse Harem Romance

Good Boys and Millionaires
Good Boys and Millionaires 1
Good Boys and Millionaires 2

Grimalkin Needs Brides
Ekpen (Intergalactic Dating Agency)
Torao (Intergalactic Dating Agency)
Leo (Intergalactic Dating Agency)

Honeypot Babies
The Polar Bear's Baby
The Jaguar's Baby
The Tiger's Baby

Honeypot Darlings
The Bear's Virgin Darling
The Bear's Virgin Mate
The Bear's Virgin Bride

Office Gentlemen
Ben From Accounting

Polar Bears of the Air Force
Staff Sergeant Polar Bear
Master Sergeant Polar Bear
Airman Polar Bear
Senior Airman Polar Bear

Return to Dragon Isle
Dragons Are Forever

Dragon Crushed: An Enemies-to-Lovers Paranormal Romance
Dragon's Hex
Dragon's Gain
Dragon's Rush

Shifters at Law
Wolf Case
Bearly Legal
Tiger Clause
Sergeant Bear
Dragon Law

Shifters of Rawr County
The Polar Bear's Fake Mate
The Lion's Fake Wife
The Tiger's Fake Date
The Wolf's Pretend Mate
The Tiger's Pretend Husband
The Dragon's Fake Fiancée
The Red Panda's Fake Mate

Stormy Mountain Bears
The Lumberjack's Baby Bear
The Writer's Baby Bear
The Mountain Man's Baby Bears

Sweet Nightmares
Sweet Nightmares: The Vampire's Melody
The Sound of Roses

Team Shifter
Bears VS Wolves
No Fox Given

The Fablestone Clan
Dragon's Oath
Dragon's Breath
Dragon's Darling
Dragon's Whisper
Dragon's Magic

The Feisty Dragons
Untamed Dragon
Naughty Dragon
Monster Dragon

The Hidden Planet

Vanquished
Outlaw
Conquered

The Wolfe City Pack
The Wolf's Darling
The Wolf's Mate
The Wolf's Bride

Standalone
Saucy Devil
Billionaire on Top
Jurassic Submissive
The Editor
Alien Beast
Snow White and the Wolves
Kissing the Billionaire
Wild
Alien Dragon
The Royal Her
Be My Tiger
Alien Monster
The Luck of the Wolves
Honeypot Babies Omnibus Edition
Honeypot Darlings: Omnibus Edition
The Swan's Mate

The Feisty Librarian
Polar Bears of the Air Force
Wild Goose Chase
Star Princess
The Virgin and the Lumberjacks
Resting Bear Face
By Hook or by Wolf
I Dare You, King
Shifters at Law
Pretty Little Fairies
Seized by the Dragon
The Fablestone Clan: A Paranormal Dragon-Shifter Romance
Collection
Star Kissed
Big Bad Academy
Club Kitten Omnibus
Stormy Mountain Bears: The Complete Collection
Bitten by the Vampires
Beautiful Villain
Dark Favors
Savored
Vampire Kiss
Chaotic Wild: A Vampire Romance
Bitten
Heartless
The Dragon's Christmas Treasure
Out of the Woods
Bullies of Crescent Academy
Craving You: A Contemporary Romance Collection
Chasing Whiskey

The Hidden Planet Trilogy
The Bratty Dom
Tokyo Wolf
The Single Dad Who Stole My Heart
Free For Him
The Feline Gaze
Fate High School
Dragon Beast: A Beauty and the Beast Retelling
Boulder Bear
Megan Slays Vampires
Once Upon a Shift: A Paranormal Romantic Comedy
Red: A Wolf Shifter Romance

www.ingramcontent.com/pod-product-compliance
Lightning Source LLC
Chambersburg PA
CBHW071754150726
47998CB00005B/1932